'I Wish I Could Understand Your Mood,'

she almost snapped. This situation was too intimate, the surroundings too romantic . . . and Paul's magnetism far too powerful.

'My mood?' Paul slanted an eyebrow and added smoothly, 'I'm sure you know that I'm in a mood to kiss you—' The next moment she was in his arms, her mouth possessed by demanding lips in a long and passionate kiss that left her fighting for breath. . . .

'Come live with me,' he quoted in a low voice. 'Emma, you need me as much as I need you, so don't throw away the pleasure you'll have. . . .'

ANNE HAMPSON

currently makes her home in England, but this top romance author has traveled and lived all over the world. This variety of experience is reflected in her books, which present the ever-changing face of romance as it is found wherever people fall in love.

Dear Reader:

I'd like to take this opportunity to thank you for all your support and encouragement of Silhouette Romances.

Many of you write in regularly, telling us what you like best about Silhouette, which authors are your favorites. This is a tremendous help to us as we strive to publish the best contemporary romances possible.

All the romances from Silhouette Books are for you, so enjoy this book and the many stories to come. I hope you'll continue to share your thoughts with us, and invite you to write to us at the address below:

Karen Solem
Editor-in-Chief
Silhouette Books
P.O. Box 769
New York, N.Y. 10019

ANNE HAMPSON
Spell of the Island

Silhouette Romance
Published by Silhouette Books New York
America's Publisher of Contemporary Romance

SILHOUETTE BOOKS, a Division of Simon & Schuster, Inc.
1230 Avenue of the Americas, New York, N.Y. 10020

ISBN: 0-671-57232-6

First Silhouette Books printing July, 1983

10 9 8 7 6 5 4 3 2 1

Map by Ray Lundgren

Other Silhouette Books by Anne Hampson

Payment in Full
Stormy Masquerade
Second Tomorrow
The Dawn Steals Softly
Man of the Outback
Where Eagles Nest
Man Without a Heart
Shadow of Apollo
Enchantment
Fascination
Desire
Realm of the Pagans
Man Without Honour
Stardust
A Kiss and a Promise
Devotion
Strangers May Marry
The Tender Years
To Buy a Memory
Another Eden
When Love Comes
Dreamtime
Love So Rare
The Dawn Is Golden
Sweet Second Love

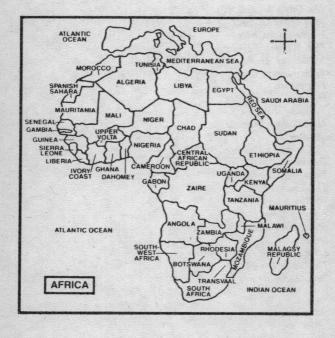

ATLANTIC OCEAN

EUROPE

N

MEDITERRANEAN SEA

MOROCCO

TUNISIA

ALGERIA

LIBYA

EGYPT

SAUDI ARABIA

SPANISH SAHARA

MAURITANIA

MALI

NIGER

CHAD

SUDAN

RED SEA

SENEGAL

GAMBIA

GUINEA

SIERRA LEONE

LIBERIA

UPPER VOLTA

NIGERIA

CENTRAL AFRICAN REPUBLIC

ETHIOPIA

IVORY COAST

GHANA

DAHOMEY

CAMEROON

SOMALIA

UGANDA

KENYA

GABON

ZAIRE

TANZANIA

MAURITIUS

ATLANTIC OCEAN

ANGOLA

ZAMBIA

MALAWI

SOUTH-WEST AFRICA

RHODESIA

MOZAMBIQUE

MALAGSY REPUBLIC

BOTSWANA

TRANSVAAL

SOUTH AFRICA

INDIAN OCEAN

AFRICA

Chapter One

Mrs. Morris was crying when Emma phoned her.

'I'm sorry, dear,' she choked across the line. 'Can you ring later—?'

'What's wrong?' broke in Emma concernedly. 'You sound very distressed.'

'It's Louise. She's become so unhappy—please ring later,' begged the woman, and to Emma's surprise she put down the phone.

Standing, staring at the receiver in her hand, Emma realised that her heart was beating far too quickly. And without further ado, she determined to find out what was wrong with the woman who, twenty-two years ago, had fostered her out at the age of two, and along with her husband, now dead, had nurtured Emma with all the loving care of real parents.

Louise . . . Emma's thoughts were naturally on the girl who had been born to Emma's foster parents only a year after they had taken Emma, after having been assured by the doctor that they could never have a child of their own. Both girls had received love, and both had given love in return, so that the three women were still very close, with Emma visiting her 'mother' as she had always called her, at least once a fortnight. Emma worked in London; her mother lived in Cheshire so it was a drive of two hundred fifty miles each way when she went to visit Mrs. Morris. But Emma tried not to miss a visit, not after Louise had taken the post of nanny on the island of Mauritius in the Indian Ocean. She had been away from home now for over a year, but two months ago her employers had moved to Sri Lanka where Mr. Winnick was to work for three years; and they had left Louise with the little boy, but moved her from their house to that of Mrs. Winnick's brother—'an arrogant blanc Mauritian who considers me a fool as regards intelligence and an especially inefficient nanny.' This from Louise about a month ago, and there was more which Emma read between the lines and hoped her mother did not also perceive—that Louise was far from happy now that she was under the watchful eye of a man she obviously detested.

All the same, it had not struck Emma that the situation would worsen; on the contrary, she had assumed that this man would soon lose interest and go about his business, allowing Louise to go about hers.

Now, it seemed trouble loomed, and Mrs. Morris was plainly taking things very much to heart.

It was fortunate that Emma was on a week's vacation, having taken it in order to decorate her tiny flat. She was papering her bedroom but left it after the phone call, and within a couple of hours she was on her way, speeding along the Motorway, eye on the mirror as she was, in her anxiety, exceeding the seventy-mile-an-hour limit.

Mrs. Morris gaped on opening the door of her Council house and seeing Emma standing there, suitcase in hand.

'What—?'

'Don't look so surprised, darling,' broke in Emma with a smile. 'Surely you knew I'd come?'

'But aren't you working?' Mrs. Morris opened the door wider for Emma to enter the narrow hallway. Emma put down her case at the bottom of the stairs.

She explained how she came to be off work; then she and her mother were in the living-room, and Emma was listening intently to Mrs. Morris, who although she several times said that Emma would understand it all once she had read Louise's last letter, for the present made no attempt to go upstairs to get it. Plainly she was upset, her eyes still swollen from tears much more recent than those she had been shedding when she was answering Emma's call.

'She says she can't stand it any longer—he's a dreadful man by all accounts! But the trouble is she can't come home because of the little boy—'

'She can ask this man to get someone else,' interrupted Emma, angry that her mother should be upset like this by a man she had not even met.

'She has, and he refuses, telling her arrogantly

that she signed for two years and she must stay at least that long.' Mrs. Morris went towards the kitchen door. 'I'll make some coffee and then fetch Louise's letter for you to read.'

'Can't I make the coffee?' Emma went past her and filled the kettle, looking round at what was so familiar. Poor but happy, the Morris family had been, and the death of Mr. Morris had been the first blow, reducing the family to three. Then Emma had been faced with moving to London with her firm or losing her job as secretary to the managing director. As Louise was at home at that time Emma, rather reluctantly, decided to live in London. Then Louise had gone. . . .

Emma had not expected her to leave her mother alone; it had upset Emma, and she had contemplated asking her mother to come to London to share the flat. But Mrs. Morris had roots here in the Cheshire village of Comberbach so Emma had not asked her to leave.

'Here's the letter.' Mrs. Morris had gone for it while Emma was making the coffee. And now they were both sitting by the fire drinking it, while Emma read and re-read the letter, aware of something she could not fathom, but *sure* her sister's mind had been dwelling on some additional aspect all the time she was writing the letter.

'What do you make of it?' asked Emma at last as she folded the three sheets of paper and put them back in the envelope. She was watching her mother closely and soon realised that the underlying element in the letter had completely escaped her notice. The printed word only had caused the tears and anxiety, but for Emma, well, there was an uncomfortable conviction that there was a great deal more than Louise had revealed.

'I can only think one thing: that this hateful creature is out to harass Louise at every turn; he dislikes her intensely and makes her life a sheer misery because of it.'

Emma said puzzledly, 'But why should he harass her when he knows she has a job to do? He must know she can't do it properly if he's complaining all the time.'

'Well, she says he's complaining all the time—you've just read it for yourself. And she says he treats her with contempt and sometimes seems to be sneering at her, or secretly laughing at her.' A pause and a frown and then, 'Why should he laugh at her, I wonder?'

'That,' commented Emma as she reached for her cup, 'is one thing that baffles me.'

'It can't be pleasant to be laughed at any more than it is to be admonished for not doing your job properly.'

'Louise hadn't been a nanny before she went out there,' mused Emma, her brow creased in thought as she recalled her asking Louise if she really thought she could do a job like that. Louise had never taken to children in the way Emma had, although she was always charming to them. It was just that she had never had the inclination to play with them as Emma had, when, for instance, one of Mrs. Morris's friends had called, bringing her grandchildren with her.

'She's been quite satisfactory up till the time Mr. and Mrs. Winnick went away to Sri Lanka. It's only since she went to this abominable man's home that she's been so unhappy.' Tears stood out on Mrs.

Morris's lashes, and Emma bit her lip. What was to be done? she wondered, wishing the island was not so far away.

'Louise doesn't say specifically what the man's complaints are,' she commented, recalling one particular passage in the letter.

'I'm desperately unhappy, and cry at night when I'm in bed. I never thought when I took the post, that it would bring such heartbreak. . . .'

No wrapping it up this time. Louise was obviously distraught; for otherwise she would surely have spared her mother, knowing as she did just how easily she could be upset.

'I believe he just wants to make my poor child's life a misery—' Mrs. Morris found a handkerchief to dry her eyes.

'And yet he won't let her leave?'

'That's a puzzle in itself.'

Slowly Emma took the letter out again. Just *what* was it that lay hidden within the dejection that ran the whole way through the pages?

'Do you know,' she murmured almost to herself, 'I'm not at all convinced that Louise *wants* to leave.'

'You're—!' Mrs. Morris stared, wide-eyed. 'Of course she wants to leave! She says so.'

Emma nodded her head.

'Yes,' she agreed, 'she does.'

Before her mother could comment, there was a knock on the front door, and Emma rose from her chair. It was the postman, who always gave a little rap on the panel after dropping letters through the box.

Another from Louise. . . . A sigh escaped Emma, wondering why her sister had not written to her instead of her mother. But in all the time Louise had been away she had written only four letters to Emma. Emma had put it down to her being too busy, but she herself wrote regularly once a month whether she received a reply or not.

'Oh . . . !' Mrs. Morris seemed not to want to accept the envelope held out to her by Emma. 'You open it, love,' she begged, a sob in her voice.

Emma did as she was requested, hoping against hope that something more cheerful would be enclosed in the thin airmail envelope. But she was disappointed. In fact, Louise seemed more distraught than before . . . and still Emma somehow gained the impression that the girl did not want to leave Mauritius and come home.

Reluctantly she began to read aloud, glancing now and then at her mother and swallowing a lump in her throat when even yet again tears appeared.

'Why doesn't she just walk out?' Emma's voice was sharp and angry. 'No one can force her to stay.' No, this Mauritian could not force her to stay. . . .

'She's frightened of him, it's plain,' cried Mrs. Morris. 'He's probably threatened to prosecute her if she breaks the contract!'

'I can't see him doing a thing like that.'

Her mother looked at her.

'You seem convinced that she doesn't really want to leave. But you have nothing to go on, have you?'

'Nothing concrete, no,' admitted Emma, but again she was telling herself that if Louise really wanted to leave she could do so.

'Would you leave a little boy, if you'd promised his parents you'd take good care of him while they were away?'

'She'd be leaving him with his uncle—'

'That's not an answer to my question, Emma. Would you shirk—do the dirty on your employers?'

Emma gave a sigh. For herself, she wouldn't let her employers down, but neither would she suffer as Louise was suffering. She would certainly make a concerted effort to hold her own against the wretched man.

'No,' she owned at last, 'I don't suppose I would.'

'So you can understand Louise's position. She has to put up with this for at least another year.' The sob in Mrs. Morris's voice was plain to Emma, who was suddenly angry with Louise despite what the girl was going through. Why, she asked again, hadn't Louise written to *her* instead?

'What's to be the end of it?' quivered Mrs. Morris. 'She'll be a nervous wreck long before she's free to leave.'

'I'll write to her if you like,' suggested Emma.

'And what good will that do?' was the swift rejoinder, and a lengthy silence ensued.

Emma drank her coffee, watching her mother's changing expression. It seemed an idea had come to her, decided Emma, but was certainly not prepared to hear her say, 'Can you go over there, Emma, and investigate? You've almost all your holidays still to come. . . .' Her voice trailed as Emma's expression changed. 'If it's the cost you're thinking about,' she continued before Emma could speak, 'then forget it. I have savings and I'm willing to spend some of them on the fare.'

'Mother, it's not practical to spend your money in this way,' she began, then stopped. She herself had ample money saved for the fare. . . .

'It's the only sensible thing to do, to ease my mind,' insisted her mother firmly. 'I can't go on like this, Emma. You know how easily I give way to nerves. Please, dear, do this for me,' she ended quiveringly.

Do this for me. . . . Not much to ask after all she has done for me, thought Emma, and she gave her mother a swift smile.

'All right, darling, if it's really what you want.'

'You're a real daughter to me, Emma—'

'No gratitude,' said Emma quickly. 'It is *I* who am grateful to *you.*'

'When can you go?' was the next question, and again before Emma could answer, 'You still have three weeks, I think?'

'That's right.'

'You couldn't have them tacked on to this present week? I mean, you've only had three days. . . .'

'You want me to go at once?'

'Is that possible?'

'If I can get a flight.' Emma paused a moment. 'I'm not sure that my boss'll let me off, but I'll phone him and see what he says.' Emma doubted she could get away in less than a week at least.

'Tell him it's an emergency, love.'

Emma forced a smile. She had practically arranged to have one of her weeks with a friend in the Lake District, intending to stay with her mother for a few days on the way there and again on the way back.

'Yes,' she said as she realised the tension in her mother's face. 'I'll tell him it's an emergency.' She looked at her, thinking that she was definitely aging these days, with the once lovely brown hair—almost

the same colour as Emma's and with the same
auburn tints—almost completely grey, and the once
clear skin beginning to wrinkle and fade. The hands,
too, were loose-skinned, the knuckle bones more
prominent. Emma gave a small sigh and wished she
could put back the clock.

'Will you stay tonight with me?' Mrs. Morris was
pleading; Emma said at once that she had meant to
stay.

'I brought my suitcase,' she added as a reminder.

'Did you, love? I hadn't noticed.'

'It's by the stairs. Surely you didn't suppose I'd
come up and go back in one day?'

'No, it was silly of me, for you never do. I don't
know what I'm doing half my time,' she added
frowningly. 'My mind's concentrated on one thing
only—the plight of my poor child.'

Emma knew she would never ever forget that
pulse-stopping moment when she was introduced to
Paul Fanchette. She had previously sent Louise a
telegram, and there had been no time for a reply.
Louise evinced neither surprise nor puzzlement
when she met Emma at Plaisance Airport and drove
her to the Chateau Fanchette, set on a prominence
from where the view was to a semicircular beach and
sapphire blue lagoon where multicoloured sails gave
evidence of luxury yachts and other craft.

'You don't seem surprised at my rather hasty
decision to come over and see you,' observed Emma
who had merely said in the cable that she felt like
seeing Louise and the island on which she worked.

'I rather thought that eventually you'd get round

to visiting me here. I did describe how beautiful it was.'

No mention of what was troubling her, and at present no sign of anxiety on her lovely, fragile-like features. Fair and slender, with big blue eyes and pale but lovely skin, Louise had always inspired gentleness in her boyfriends, whereas Emma with her dark hair and expressive brown eyes, had mainly had boyfriends who seemed to take it for granted that she could fend for herself. The firm chin and high cheekbones denoted a sort of classical strength of character, though the mouth was full and tender, compassionate and could tremble if its owner were hurt. Slender like Louise, Emma was an inch taller—a little above medium height—and she supposed this, too, made men think she had no need of protection. But Emma basically was soft and at times, very vulnerable; she felt more deeply than Louise but was able more easily to hide her feelings.

However, as they drove from the airport, Louise was undoubtedly hiding her feelings, though she must know that her mother would have confided in Emma; and, therefore, Emma knew of the trouble in which she, Louise, was in with her new employer.

It was on the glorious, wide lawn that Emma first met Paul Fanchette, a lawn manicured to perfection and like a thick-pile carpet to the feet. He was merely standing there, staring out to the lagoon where, Emma was later to learn, his luxury yacht was moored.

'He's there—er—Monsieur Fanchette. . . .' Louise seemed to falter for a fleeting moment but recovered so swiftly that her sister never even noticed. In fact her eyes were already glued to the tall, lithe figure whose very pose seemed to brand him a scion of the French nobility. 'I suppose I'd better introduce you at once. I've said we're sisters, but you have a different name because you were fostered. I don't think he was really interested.' Louise led the way, adding over her shoulder, 'I said I could get you into an hotel, but he said you could stay here—but I've told you this already,' she added as if impatient with herself for the repetition.

The next moment Emma's hand was in a firm grasp that made her wince, and she was tilting her head right back to look into the most formidable countenance she had ever seen. No wonder Louise was afraid of him! He seemed like a god, so incredibly tall and distinguished but with features so set and stern that even Emma was overawed in his presence. He was dressed in white linen slacks and a white shirt with rolled-up sleeves, revealing teak dark arms to match the colour of his face. His raven hair was formed into a widow's peak at the front and brushed back, waving slightly, from his forehead. One or two threads of silver at the temples accentuated the air of distinction, just as the hollows in his cheeks accentuated the high cheekbones and straight, aristocratic nose. His mouth was firm but somehow sensuous at the same time, full . . . too full. . . . Emma swallowed hard to relieve the dryness in her throat. Never in her entire life had she been affected like this by a man. It was absurd, she chided herself, for she had not been in his presence more than a mere few seconds!

'How do you do, Miss Carpenter?' he said, subjecting her to the keenest scrutiny she had ever known. His dark eyes seemed to take in everything about her face before travelling downwards . . . to rest for one interested moment on the firm outline of her breasts. She coloured delicately, was aware of her sister's narrowed gaze and made a supreme effort to compose herself. 'You had a good flight?' The suave voice was finely-timbred and low.

'Yes, thank you,' murmured Emma, vitally conscious of the cool strength of the hand which still held hers.

'Welcome to the chateau,' said the suave voice, while the eyes seemed to have locked themselves to Emma's. 'I hope you have an enjoyable holiday.' He paused, releasing her hand. 'How long shall you be staying?'

So formal! There was a formidable rigidity about him that made Emma wonder if he ever unbent.

'About a fortnight,' answered Emma, 'or perhaps a little longer.' She had at first suggested to her mother that she should spend only a week here, leaving herself some further holidays but after a discussion it was decided that Emma should stay at least a fortnight. The fare was expensive so it was not logical to have a mere seven days on the lovely island.

'You haven't been to this part of the world before?' His eyes had moved. And he was staring out to the lagoon again, just as if he had had enough of the two girls, thought Emma.

'No, this is my first visit abroad in fact.'

'I'll not keep you,' he said after a pause during which he gave Emma his attention again, his eyes roving her figure and his mouth curving in a sort of mocking amusement when he saw he was embarrassing her.

A womaniser! No doubt about it, decided Emma. And yet, why hadn't he given Louise some attention? 'Miss Morris, take your sister to her room.' The order was brusquely spoken, and the look he gave her was one of cool indifference.

'What do you think of him?' Louise wanted to know once they were in the lovely mauve and cream room Emma was to have.

'A strange man . . .'

'With striking looks.'

'He's certainly handsome despite the austere features and hard eyes.' Emma paused momentarily. 'How are you getting on with him, Louise?'

Silence, with Louise staring hard at her sister.

'I expect Mother's told you how I feel—and that's why you're here, isn't it?'

Emma nodded her head, rather glad that Louise had made the intelligent guess as to the reason for her coming out to the island.

'Yes, it is. Mother's dreadfully troubled about you, Louise. You shouldn't have let her know just how unhappy you are.' Emma's tone was critical and Louise pouted. She's changed, discovered Emma in astonishment.

'I couldn't help it; I was feeling as low as could be when I sent those letters.'

'Perhaps,' suggested Emma lifting her suitcase on to the bed, 'you ought to explain.'

Louise looked at her from where she stood with her back to the high, wide window behind which was a balcony dripping with exotic flowers growing in earthenware pots.

'He's awful with me,' began Louise when Emma interrupted her.

'I have gathered that. But there must be more to it. Why should this Monsieur Fanchette take such a strong dislike to you?'

'You feel there's a good reason?'

Emma shrugged and threw back the lid of the case.

'It's not normal for someone to act as he does without reason.' She lifted a lapis blue evening dress from its tissue paper and laid it on the bed.

'What reason did you have in mind, Emma?' inquired Louise, and Emma started in surprise, turning to her questioningly.

'That's a strange thing to ask,' was all she could find to say.

'I can tell by your manner that you feel instinctively that Paul must have a good reason for the way he treats me.'

'Paul?'

It was Louise's turn to shrug impatiently. She looked sulky, observed Emma with an inward sigh. Just what *was* the matter? She had been sent to find out; she had hoped to be able to do something positive—though for the life of her she could not figure out what—in order to be able to reassure her mother on her return.

'I don't call him Paul to his face—I'd never dare! But I naturally always think of him as Paul.'

'You do?' in some surprise. 'I don't think I would—not if I were in your position.' Another dress was shaken from its soft wrapping, and now Emma put them both in the wardrobe. The other one was a lovely creation of citrus green with rather sexy tight-fitting bodice and full flared skirt. The neckline was rather low, but along with the antique silver necklace which was her mother's twenty-first birthday present to her, it looked a million dollars!—or so one of Emma's boyfriends had said. Somehow, Emma did not think she would wear it while she was here.

'A servant?' from Louise shortly. She turned and looked out at the lovely gardens where fountains played and bright tropical fish swam in the pool below. 'I don't consider myself as a servant. A nanny's job is different. Nannies usually eat with the parents of the child. I did when I was with the Winnicks.'

'This man is different, then?'

'You know very well he is! He treats me like dirt!'

Emma turned from her unpacking and stared at her sister's back.

'Are you sure you've done nothing to offend him?' she inquired tentatively, and Louise swung around, anger in her big, blue eyes.

'What makes you ask a question like that?' she demanded.

There was a short silence before Emma spoke. She was extremely perplexed, and a little frustrated as well. There was something deep here, but she knew for sure she would get nothing out of her sister.

'It occurred to me, that's all,' she returned and went on with her unpacking.

Louise glanced at her watch.

'I'll have to go and pick up Jeremy from school,' she sighed. 'Are you coming with me? It's only about twenty minutes there and back in the car.'

Emma shook her head.

'I'll finish this if you don't mind. And then I'd like to take a bath and change my clothes.'

'All right.' Louise moved to the door. 'I'll see you later,' she added and went out.

Emma stared at the closed door for fully thirty seconds, her thoughts on the conversation they had just had. And then with a sigh of impatience, she hurried through her unpacking, and as she went to the dressing-room to put away the suitcase, her eyes wandered to the window. It looked so peaceful out there that she postponed the bath and decided on a stroll in the garden.

Once out in the grounds she realised that Monsieur Fanchette had his own private beach. But she left that exploration for another time and wandered along a secluded path instead. And suddenly she found herself almost face-to-face with the owner of the chateau.

He was coming towards her as she took a bend in the path, and quite illogically she wanted to turn and run from him. But of course she did nothing of the kind, and soon he had stopped, fully blocking the path. Emma felt as if her legs were made of rubber, and she frowned in sheer annoyance, for she did think she was behaving like a shy schoolgirl who has suddenly become aware that she has a crush on someone.

Colour was sweeping into her face, and her long,

curling lashes were lowered, sending exquisite shadows onto her hot cheeks. She was deeply affected by the man but hoped she did not show it.

'So we meet again,' he remarked with a sort of satirical amusement. 'Where is your sister?'

'Gone for Jeremy,' briefly and with a side-stepping attempt to pass him. To her amazement he moved at the same time and again her escape route was blocked. He was close, towering above her, his dark eyes kindling in a way that set the nerves tingling in her veins. It was so quiet here, and lonely—quite a distance from the chateau.

'You didn't go with her,' he commented unnecessarily. 'Decided to take a stroll instead, eh?' The accented voice almost held a sneer, and Emma frowned in puzzlement. 'Did you happen to see me taking a walk?'

'You—! No, what do you mean?' There was only *one* meaning, she thought, and now it was anger that set her cheeks on fire.

'It seems that there are two of you—but you're a little different, more to my taste—' Without giving Emma the slightest sign of what he intended, he had caught her wrist, jerked her to him, lifted her chin and his lips were imprisoning hers in a long and passionate kiss. 'Satisfied?' he inquired imperturbably when at length he held her from him. She was shaking, not only with fury but also with the effects of that kiss.

It had affected her so greatly that she had almost reciprocated!

'Leave go of me!' she blazed, having the greatest difficulty in not kicking his shin. 'You—you—scoundrel!' She could think of a stronger word, but to her intense relief she managed not to utter it. 'What's the idea, molesting me—a stranger!'

He released her but continued to block her path.

'Stranger or old acquaintance—women are all the same.' His voice and eyes held contempt. 'Your sister's rather more of a bore than the rest, though. She's determined to keep trying.'

'My sister?' echoed Emma, for the moment diverted. 'You mean—she—she runs—' Abruptly she stopped, but her companion finished the sentence for her.

'. . . after me? All the time,' he added through his teeth. And then as if the idea had just occurred to him, 'Perhaps you can do something—give her some advice—'

'What kind of advice?' cut in Emma, recalling her impression that something subtle underlay the words of Louise's letters. She was attracted to this man . . . and despite her unhappiness she could not bear to leave his house.

'You have me there,' was his surprising admission, and now he appeared to be amused. 'The girl's mad for a man—'

'What a thing to say!' Emma's fists were tight; he glanced down at them and for a long, tense moment the very air around them seemed to be electrically charged.

'Anger . . . I find you attractive when you're like this—'

'Shut up!' she fumed, glowering at him. 'What an opinion you have of yourself—believing every woman you meet is running after you!' Her dark eyes raked his entire length in contempt. 'For me—I'd not have you if you were the last man on earth!'

He laughed in sheer amusement. Looking up at him, Emma caught her breath. The man was too darned attractive by far! No man should possess this kind of superlative good looks!

'If I were the last man on earth,' he said, laughter still in his eyes, 'you wouldn't stand a chance.'

She gasped at his audacity, not realising that he was finding her diverting, and he was thoroughly enjoying this little sparring match with her.

'Your ego certainly needs deflating!' she snapped. Then added for good measure, 'I'd love to be the one to do it.'

The dark eyes were dancing as they looked down into hers. And once again she was taken by surprise, jerked to his hard body and kissed with almost brutal passion. His mouth was warm and moist, possessive, masterful, demanding reciprocation. Emma fought valiantly, but the man's powerful attraction had already made itself felt, affecting her from the very moment she had set eyes on him. She felt the deliberate thrust of his tongue and opened her mouth, shuddering with near rapture at the roughness against her flesh. His hands were not idle, either; he stroked her cheek, gently letting his long, brown fingers slide downwards to caress her shoulder beneath the open neckline of her blouse. And only when his warm, strong hand enclosed her breast did she cast off the languour of submission and try to push him away. He was expecting such a move, he'd learned from experience, she thought with a sort of growing bitterness. And she was held in a hawser-strong grip while he again took his fill of her lips. The hand on her breast hurt a little, by its strength, but the quiver that passed through her was one of pleasure. Again he knew what to expect. A low laugh escaped him, triumphant and contemptuous. He held her away at last and, looking into her dreamy eyes, said with mocking satire, 'Yes, you're all the same, following the pattern.' He released her and was suddenly suppressing a yawn, an action that ignited a fury so strong that she did no more than lift a hand to slap his face. But before that satisfaction could be achieved her wrist was caught, and she uttered a little cry of pain.

'You—brute!' she blazed, struggling like a wildcat to gain her freedom. 'I hate you—and I'm not staying here another moment! I'll go to an hotel!' She looked down at the wrist he had at last released; the bruise made her see red, and again she lifted her hand. But this time she dropped it swiftly because of the expression on his face.

'Yes,' he said slowly as he watched the action, 'you are very wise. I'd have given you something to remember if you'd made your target.'

She knew just what he meant and turned away. This time he allowed her to pass, and she moved quickly, his low laugh like the sound of a rasp in her ears.

Chapter Two

Emma very naturally refrained from telling Louise what had happened, and this meant that she, Emma, could not go out and find an hotel. Fury mingled with humiliation, for she was sure she could have struggled and escaped before he managed to excite her, arouse her emotions to the point where she was submitting. Obviously he was aware of his power over women; they were all the same, he said. They followed a pattern.

And because of it, he was bored with them. . . .

But one day he would find one who did not bore him and then, she surmised, he would marry. And surprisingly, as she thought about it, she found herself believing that he would be faithful! Incredible as it seemed—yes—when he had found *the* one, it would be the end of philandering for him.

'You're very quiet,' observed her sister, and Emma glanced up from her plate. It was dinnertime and they were eating in the little sitting-room which had been allocated to Louise. Jeremy had had his tea and been put to bed. Noticing Louise's impatience with the child, Emma, feeling sorry for the little boy who was only five and a half, went into his bedroom and read him a story. A bright, intelligent child, he listened attentively, eyes sparkling and hands sometimes clutching the bedcover.

'That was great!' he said when at length she closed the book after promising to read him another story tomorrow night. 'I like stories about pirates!'

Louise had gone to her room, and when she emerged and joined Emma she looked as glamorous as if she were dining out and going to a show afterwards. Emma opened her mouth to express her surprise but closed it again.

It was plain that Louise was looking her best just in case she should come into contact with Paul Fanchette.

Emma had decided on a cotton dress, flowered on a background of pale blue. The neck was low—in fact the bodice was held up only by shoulder straps—since the dress was really designed as a sundress. Emma had washed her hair and it glowed—softly brown and deep auburn tinted.

'Quiet?' she repeated, looking at Louise across the table. 'I was thinking of your boss, as a matter of fact.'

'Don't refer to him as my boss!' flashed Louise sharply. 'The Winnicks are my employers!'

'Sorry.' Emma counted ten. 'There's no need to be so shirty with me, though.'

'You don't understand. . . .' Louise choked on her food, and her lower lip quivered. 'You don't understand anything.'

'Then help me to understand,' invited Emma encouragingly. 'You know how troubled Mother is, and she'll be expecting some kind of reassurance when I get back home.'

'He hates me!' was all Louise vouchsafed in answer to that, and Emma drew an exasperated breath.

'What has caused this—well—rift between you and Monsieur Fanchette?'

There was a long pause before her sister spoke.

'He disliked me from the very first—'

'You haven't answered my question,' persisted Emma, half-inclined to reveal what she knew.

But the next moment, and after a further period of hesitation, Louise said quiveringly, 'I've fallen madly in love with him, Emma, and I'm being crucified by his treatment of me.'

Emma swallowed to moisten the dryness in her throat. She had not supposed it was as bad as this. She had suspected no more than a crush, an emotional experience resulting from the superlative attractions of the Mauritian. But as she stared at Louise, noting the despairing droop to the lovely mouth, the dark misery in the blue eyes, Emma was left in no doubt at all that her sister was genuinely in love with the man who treated her with contempt, believing she was running after him . . . which she had been doing, thought Emma with a heavy frown.

'The best thing you can do is leave here,' decided Emma at length. 'This situation can't possibly continue. Besides, when Jeremy's parents come back you wouldn't be seeing Monsieur Fanchette anyway—at least, not very often.'

Louise stared mistily at her, having pushed her plate away.

'I just keep on hoping he'll change,' she admitted, a sob in her voice. 'Miracles do happen, and you hear of men disliking women and later falling wildly in love with them.'

'It doesn't happen very often. In any case, this man's an experienced womaniser who seems always to have had women running after him; it's made him regard himself as something very special—'

'He is something special.' Louise made the interruption, because she couldn't help it, but she coloured up immediately the words were spoken.

'I suppose I have to agree,' returned Emma, but grudgingly. 'Nevertheless, he's a nasty piece of work, with a head the size of a balloon and an inflated opinion of himself in general. He's plainly of the opinion that every woman he meets wants him to make love to her—craves his caresses, in fact. Well, Louise, he just isn't worth a thought, so you'll be wise to write him off and come back home with me.' Already Louise was shaking her head.

'What about Jeremy?' she said.

Remembering Louise's near impatience with the child at bedtime—for clearly she was glad to be rid of him—Emma said quietly, 'I don't think you are really concerned with that aspect, are you, Louise?' and before she could answer, Emma was adding in the same quiet tone of voice, 'Once you've given the man a fortnight's notice he'll begin looking for a replacement—'

'I can't leave!' cried her sister unhappily. 'I've already told you I'm hoping for a change in Paul's attitude towards me.'

'Throwing yourself at him won't bring about a change.' Emma felt inclined to be callous, for she desperately wanted Louise to come home with her in a fortnight's time. 'He's the kind of man who'll naturally treat with utter contempt any woman who tries to gain his attention.'

'You're so knowledgeable!' snapped Louise, and Emma did think just how she had changed. Was this what unrequited love did for you?

I'll take darned good care it never happens to me, declared Emma but to herself . . . and yet as she silently formed the sentence there arose before her the image of Paul Fanchette . . . debonair and handsome, confident, egotistical. . . .

She set her teeth on remembering the scene of just a couple of hours ago, temper rising as she recalled her own reaction, the arousal of emotions she would rather not think about.

Undoubtedly the man was a menace to women, and she was determined to keep him at a distance during her stay here in his home.

Emma and Louise talked for some time without any headway being made as regards Emma's practical solution to the problem. Louise was not giving up; she was in the depths of despair and yet, conversely, cherishing the optimistic hope that Paul Fanchette's attitude towards her would change.

'If you don't mind, I'll go to bed now,' said Louise

when they had drunk their coffee on the verandah of Louise's sitting-room. 'I feel awful at leaving you alone, but. . . .' She tailed off on noticing her sister's perceptive expression. 'I really mean it,' she insisted with an almost belligerent look.

Emma shook her head, a gesture of impatience.

'You're going somewhere—I don't know where—hoping that detestable man will see you—'

'No, I am not!'

'Why the glamorous getup?' she wanted to know, again feeling a callous approach might just shake Louise back to her senses.

'Don't be crude, Emma! I always like to look nice for dinner! In fact, it was in your honour!'

'An explanation but not a truthful one.' Emma rose from her chair. 'Obviously you don't want me with you so I'll say good night and go to my room—'

'You make me feel rotten,' complained Louise on the edge of tears. 'You've come all this way to see me and—and this is how I treat you—' She choked suddenly and bit her lip hard to hold back the tears. 'I'm sorry, Emma, do please believe me!'

Emma was standing, and she looked down at the unhappy girl. Something had to be done . . . and Emma had now made a firm decision. . . . To her surprise Emma saw her sister go into her bedroom and although she waited on the verandah for fully ten minutes the girl did not come out.

Too upset so she had changed her mind, decided Emma and, herself, went in search of the man who was causing all the trouble. He was nowhere in the house, so she surmised he was in the garden, as his car was on the forecourt.

The night was balmy, the sky, spangled with stars.

The lagoon, lazy in the moonlight, shimmered away to where the reef rose like a miniature waterfall, making music, creating light and shade that lent an air of romance even without the swaying palms that lined the backshore. The swimming must be glorious, she mused as she wandered along one winding path and another, the dry wind rustling through a belt of tamarind trees and the spidery fronds of the palms. Her eyes searched; she was determined to talk with Paul Fanchette, and yet the thought of the encounter was causing her nerves to tense, her heart to beat a little overrate. As she continued to wander and search, she thought of the wealth and splendour of the chateau with its French furniture, its exquisite decor, its Persian carpets and rugs. Gold-plated fittings even in the guest bathroom, and she wondered what *his* was like. She had asked Louise about his line of business, learnt that he owned tea and sugarcane factories—was in fact the largest exporter on the island. Wealth as well as the supreme beneficence of Nature! And all it had done to him was inflate his ego and self-esteem, create vanity out of all proportion, unbelievable conceit and arrogance.

How on earth Louise could have fallen in love with him Emma would never understand!—for a more detestable man she had never met.

And as Emma decided this, the man under review came strolling along on the other side of a low hedge of hibiscus vines. His footsteps had been light; she was angered at being taken by surprise but managed to keep her voice steady as she said without hesitation, 'Ah, Monsieur Fanchette—I'd like a few words with you.'

'Yes.' He stopped, head and shoulders above the neatly trimmed hedge. Emma was at an immediate disadvantage since she had to tilt her head, a circumstance that only served to increase her anger. 'What about, might I ask?'

She set her teeth at the arrogance and amusement in his voice.

'We can't talk over a hedge,' was her stiff rejoinder.

'There isn't much at all one can do with a hedge between them.' Mockery in his voice, and Emma's teeth gritted together. She very much feared she would again attempt to hit out at the pompous creature!

'The talk is serious.' Quivered tones but the hope that he would not notice. 'I have something important to request of you, Monsieur. Please afford me a few moments of your time and attention. . . .' Her voice trailed to silence as he laughed.

'So stiff,' he commented. 'An armour of self-defence which some women assume, yet invariably it's a thin, ineffective cloak—'

'Would you mind keeping your observations on women for another time and audience?' broke in Emma frigidly. 'What I have to say won't take long, and then I can go to my room. I'm tired after the long flight.'

He looked at her with an odd expression . . . almost as if he were intrigued by her manner.

'Perhaps we can talk over a drink,' he suggested and with long graceful strides made for the end of the dividing foliage and was soon coming towards her. She waited, legs weak, boneless. This place was lonely . . . and only minutes ago she had decided to keep her distance. His assurance, the sensuous twist of his mouth, the dark embers that seemed to glow in his eyes . . .

Wanting to run, Emma half turned, then remembered what she had come out here for and remained where she was until he reached her side. 'You look troubled,' he observed, glancing down at her in the moonlight. 'Are you not enjoying your holiday?'

'I've only been here a few hours,' she returned shortly.

'A temper,' he remarked with unexpected offhandedness. 'Most women are similarly endowed, though they don't always practice your control. In what way have I annoyed you?' he ended and as she could scarcely say that his whole manner stuck in her gullet, she compromised by reminding him of his treatment of her a few hours previously.

'It was disgraceful,' she added, aware that she had not put much strength into her explanation, but she had no wish to antagonise him to a point where he would refuse the request she was about to make.

'You weren't noticeably averse at the time,' he returned in taunting accents. 'For myself, I thoroughly enjoyed the interlude . . . even though it was far too short.'

She gasped at the audacity of him! Then glancing up, she realised he was playing with her, deriving exceeding amusement at her expense.

She said in a glacier-cold tone of voice, 'If we can talk at once, then—'

'In the salon,' he broke in firmly.

She drew an exasperated breath which could not possibly escape his ears.

'As you wish,' she snapped, 'but let us have no more delay!'

Once in the luxurious apartment, and with a drink in her hand which she did not want but which had literally been forced upon her, Emma wasted no time in saying what was in her mind.

'It's about Louise, Monsieur Fanchette. I want you to let her leave—I really mean, I want you to dismiss her.'

Silence. He was standing by the cocktail cabinet, a glass in his hand. When he spoke his voice was terse.

'As I am not your sister's employer, I have no authority to dismiss her.'

'But you could if you so chose.' Emma's voice was coldly deliberate.

'Jeremy needs a nanny.'

'You can find a replacement.' She sent him a direct glance. 'You dislike my sister intensely; you've treated her abominably from the very first, so surely it will suit you to get her out of your house?'

'I have no intention of interfering in matters which don't concern me, Miss Carpenter.' He took a sip of his brandy. 'The matter is therefore closed.' He was a different man now, a stern and determined person whose previous manner might never have existed. No amused mockery in those hard eyes, no sardonic twist of the sensuous lips. They were firmly pressed together and the jawline was taut.

'Can you give me some explanation?' inquired Emma, already frustrated by his implacability.

'Explanation of what?'

'Your wish to keep Louise here when you dislike her so much.'

'She's obviously exaggerated my—er—dislike.'

'By your own admission you find her a bore.'

'Because of her persistence in throwing herself at me.' His mouth went tight. 'She came here as an employee but did not know how to keep her place.'

'You're talking to her sister,' seethed Emma, furious at his plain speaking. 'Has it not occurred to you that I might be embarrassed?'

He looked at her for a long moment, subjecting her to a keen and all-examining scrutiny.

'You and she are not related, she told me.'

'Can we keep to the point?' she snapped. 'I must tell you that our mother is greatly troubled because of Louise's unhappiness. I came here to see what was wrong—'

'Your sister has written to her mother about me?'

'Naturally she's told her of your treatment of her.'

'But not the reason for that treatment, obviously. However, *you* know why I dislike her—'

'Then release her!' flashed Emma, fast losing both patience and temper. 'Mother will be saved from further anxiety.'

'I'm sorry for your mother. . . .' He lifted a hand to hide a yawn, and Emma's eyes glittered at the unnecessary action. 'However, I fail to see why I should give myself the trouble of getting another nanny for my nephew when I can leave things as they are.'

'And be uncomfortable?'

His eyes opened wide.

'It would seem it's Miss Morris who is uncomfortable, not me.'

A sigh escaped her. She had been so optimistic,

assuming this man would be glad to listen to her, even though he had previously refused to let Louise go. But he was as adamant as ever; and judging by that implacable expression, Emma felt sure she would avail herself nothing by further argument. That his whole attitude was unreasonable was an undoubted fact, but obviously he was not intending to put himself to the trouble of finding a replacement for Louise.

She said presently, 'Is it possible for Louise to return to the Winnicks' home rather than stay here?'

He looked at her curiously.

'Your sister's talked to you, obviously, since you arrived here. She's denounced me as a tyrant—'

'And aren't you a tyrant?' she could not help asking.

He looked at her in some amusement.

'I am a stickler for efficiency. Your sister has neither the patience nor the experience to be a competent nanny. I have repeatedly had to admonish her for neglect—'

'Then for heaven's sake let her go!' cried Emma in exasperation. 'It's the only logical thing to do!'

'I've already said, she stays to work out her contract. After that—' he spread a hand carelessly, 'something can be arranged.'

'But why not now?'

Suddenly his eyes narrowed.

'Miss Carpenter,' he said coldly, 'I have said all I intend saying on the subject. Please let it drop.'

But Emma had to ask again if it were possible for Louise to return to the Winnicks' home. He shook his head.

'It happens to have been rented out,' he explained briefly, and Emma bit her lip.

She wanted to argue, to persist until he gave in—what a hope! This man never gave in! He was like some despot whose every word and command had to be obeyed!

At last, admitting defeat, she rose from her chair. But Paul Fanchette halted her intended departure with the very logical statement, 'If your sister is so unhappy then she herself could break the contract and leave her post.' Something subtle in the words and Emma paused, irresolute for a long moment before phrasing a reply.

'I think you know why she doesn't, Monsieur Fanchette. Louise finds you . . . attractive. . . .' She trailed off, frowning, and her companion laughed in that special way that was hateful to her ears.

'That was difficult for you, wasn't it? Your reluctance stood out a mile.'

'Just as your pomposity stands out a mile!' she retorted from her place by the door. 'Never have I met anyone so puffed up with his own importance. One day someone will bring you down to earth—and the sooner the better.' She had a hand on the brass doorknob and she turned it. 'I said I'd be here for two weeks but it won't be anywhere near that long! I have no wish to accept your hospitality, Monsieur Fanchette, and I shall be leaving immediately I can arrange a flight!' She flung wide the door, but again he halted her departure.

'You said a few hours ago you were intending to stay at an hotel, but you changed your mind, and the reason is obvious: you would have had to give your sister an explanation which, of course,' he added with amused mockery, 'you were not inclined to do. And now you threaten to leave almost immediately, but again you will have to produce some reason.' He stopped to look directly at her before resuming, 'What reason do you have, Miss Carpenter?'

She ground her teeth, temper blazing within her. Tense moments passed before she asked curiously, 'Wouldn't you be glad to see me go? I mean—' She was suddenly embarrassed. 'You dislike me as much as you dislike my sister, so—'

'I haven't expressed my dislike, nor have I given you any sign that it is as you say.'

Nerves tensed; she felt she ought to be making a speedy escape but some force beyond her control kept her where she was. This man possessed an invincible power which, she felt sure, he could at will exert over anyone he chose . . . especially over women.

'I don't think I—I understand,' she stammered, her eyes dilating as he proceeded slowly towards her, so confident that she would stay where she was. 'I—don't you d-dare touch m-me . . . !' He was already touching her, holding her wrist, painlessly but firmly for all that.

'Perhaps I can *make* you understand,' he murmured, drawing her away from the door and deliberately kicking it shut with the toe of one immaculate, patent leather shoe. 'Dislike you?' His eyes seemed to kindle with desire as he added smoothly, 'On the contrary, I find you enticingly attractive—very different from your sister who is so transparent.' Another small pause during which Emma vaguely wondered why she wasn't struggling for freedom or even threatening to scream. Instead, she merely attempted to avoid the lips that were coming down to fasten themselves to hers. But even as she averted her head, she felt a strong hand beneath her chin, and she was compelled to lift her face. His arms were about her slender frame, his mouth wide and sensuous, poised for the mastery of the victor. He was so sure of himself! And Emma felt weak and helpless . . . and already aware of rising emotions. The kiss was lacking in any kind of respect, and the roving hands seemed to hold a spell under whose influence she was swiftly falling. He caressed her nape, tormenting with unendurable mastery and persistence, while his iron-hard body pressed to hers until she felt moulded to its shape. Tremors shuddered through her frame—glorious emotional experiences which awakened a fierce, reluctant longing and set her senses strumming with erotic intensity. One hand was clasping her body tightly, while the other was now in possession of a captured breast, flesh bared, though she did not know how or when he had slipped one thin strap from her shoulder. The moist mouth was mobile and demanding, compelling her to part her lips. The thrust of his tongue sent shudders of ecstasy through every nerve cell in her being and she heard her own reluctant murmur . . . a plea . . . for what . . . ?

Her hands were resting on his shoulders; she wanted to touch his nape, spread her fingers into his hair, arch her body even closer so that she would be aware of his manhood. But a certain shyness mingled with the vague awareness that she ought not to have allowed herself to be in this position at all. But it was too late for protests and struggles as one hand slid right down over her thigh to curl itself around her lower curves, while the fingers of the other hand employed their experienced finesse in manipulating the nipple, coercing it to a hard bud of desire. The ache of longing spread into Emma's loins as erotic sensations burst into life, setting her entire body on fire. Her breathing became erratic; she knew a dryness in her mouth and throat and swallowed convulsively. He had lifted the hem of her dress, and she felt him quiver as his roving hand caressed the silk of her flesh.

'Yes,' he breathed throatily, his mouth almost buried in her shoulder, 'you're very different from your sister. I have a mind to take you, and keep you for a while. Let's go up to my room—you're trembling,' he murmured and laughed. 'It's nothing to the way you will feel in a few moments—'

'No!' At last sanity was returning, and she thrust him away, taking him by surprise. 'Oh, how could I let myself—! I hate you!' she cried, pummelling at his chest in her frenzy of temper. 'I hate you! Do you hear?'

'Cut out the hysterics,' was his heartless response as with brutal force he jerked her roughly to him again. This time his passion was so unbridled that she was carried into a raging tempest that sent her head spinning, her senses reeling, so that for several seconds she seemed to be poised on the brink of oblivion. His whipcord-hard body was all but possessing hers as his male hardness was thrust against her soft, vulnerable flesh, and the hands pressing her to him were merciless in their strength as once again, but weakly now, Emma made some attempt at escape. Shudders of ecstasy ripped through her, and she felt then that she was lost.

A cry—a plea—left her lips; she felt it was a futile attempt, but to her amazement he released the pressure and within a moment he was cool and collected—a miraculous transformation! He stood away, a twisted smile on his lips, his dark eyes narrowed as if he would conceal the passion still to be seen within their depths.

'Why did I stop?' He was asking himself the question, and he shook his head and said with the hint of a frown, 'I shall never know.' He walked away to pour himself a drink then turned, half expecting her to be gone. But instead she had sunk weakly into a chair, ashamed of her fatigue but aware that he would know of it.

'I hate you. . . .' She spoke softly and her mouth trembled. 'Just why are you doing this to me?'

For a full thirty seconds he seemed not to have an answer to her question. But at last he said, in that faintly accented voice which for some reason seemed very alien now, 'You appeal to me, physically, Emma, and—'

'Don't call me Emma!' she seethed. 'You know my name!'

He seemed amused, eyes glimmering.

'That temper again. I rather think I would like to curb it for you.'

She drew a breath.

'You'll not have the opportunity!' she assured him. 'I'm leaving here—'

'As I was saying,' he broke in casually, 'you appeal to me—more than any woman has for years. How would you like to stay for a while? You'd leave far richer than when you came.'

So cool! Emma gasped and shook her head. The man was crazed with his own importance to women!

'I'll bid you good night!' she said and rose unsteadily from the chair, conscious that desire was still affecting her nerves. The ache in her loins was still there, the thrilling sensation of his fingers on her breast.

'Sit down,' he advised, pointing to the chair. 'You're not yourself yet.'

She managed to get to the door.

'Think about my offer,' he said as she opened it. 'I rather have an idea you will accept it.'

'Then your head's bigger than I thought.' She waited, but he said nothing and she added with a curious inflection, 'You seem very serious about our having an affair, but have you visualised the situation it would create? My sister works here; she has a—well—liking for you. How would she feel? And do you suppose I'd be willing to hurt her?' She shook her head in faint bewilderment. 'You haven't considered anything, have you?'

'On the contrary,' he rejoined, 'I have considered every aspect. I would offer you a post in one of my offices in Saint Louis where I also own a delightful apartment, at present rented to a businessman, but he leaves in a week's time. You can have the post—and I'd see, of course, that your hours were very short—just for appearance sake and to put your sister off the scent, as it were, and live in the

apartment which I would refurbish for you.' His
suave voice faded as Emma shook her head in
disbelief, a gasp on her lips.

'You've worked it all out?' Again she moved her
head from side to side. 'How confident you must be!'

'I am, my dear, very confident. I can—' He
stopped abruptly, for Emma had opened the door.

'—go to hell,' she threw over her shoulder, finishing the sentence her way. And she went out, leaving
the door wide open behind her.

Chapter Three

Emma stood watching Jeremy playing ball on the lawn with one of the younger gardeners. He needs company of his own age, she thought, knowing that Louise could do much more for the child than she was doing. Was it her attitude towards Paul Fanchette that had caused her to become lax? There was certainly an essence of lethargy about her for most of the time; she had no patience with anyone these days.

'He's taking no harm.' Louise had come up behind her on the patio. 'You fuss too much, Emma. Jeremy is quite happy; he does have company at school, remember.'

'And a good thing too,' returned Emma dryly.

'You think I'm shirking my duty, don't you?'

'If you want a forthright answer, it's yes.' Emma rested her hands on the rail, her eyes pensive. Two days had passed since that unforgettable scene with Paul Fanchette, but embarrassment and humiliation still filled her being whenever she thought about it, which quite naturally was often.

She had determined to remove herself the following morning, but she could find no excuse to give her sister. She could scarcely reveal the truth, and so she decided to stay on—at least for a while—but as before, she vowed to keep out of Paul Fanchette's way.

Up till now it had been easy, since he was in his study for most of the day, but an hour or so ago he had come upon Emma and Louise and said casually, 'I'd like you two to have dinner with me this evening,' and he had moved on without affording either of them the chance to accept or reject the invitation.

Louise was in high spirits, declaring that it was her especially whom he wanted for company.

'He's been better with me these past two days—but I expect you've noticed?' she said, and Emma returned dryly, 'I haven't noticed, no. He's been in his study most of the time as far as I could see.'

'He's spoken to me several times, and not once to find fault or treat me with that awful contempt I've become used to.' Her lovely face was radiant; her big blue eyes shining. Emma sighed with impatience and wondered, not for the first time, what would be the outcome of all this.

'I wish you wouldn't attach so much importance to

this invitation,' she had said with a sigh. 'I'm very sure it means nothing.'

'It must mean something,' argued Louise, 'for otherwise he'd not have invited me to dine with him—I mean, us,' she corrected on noticing the lift of her sister's eyebrows.

Now, as she stood on the patio watching the little boy at play, Emma wondered what she was going to tell her mother when she wrote to her tomorrow. Mrs. Morris had begged her to write as soon as possible after her arrival and tell her what was wrong between Louise and her employer—for Mrs. Morris now regarded Paul Fanchette as her daughter's employer.

Emma had not been able to write, as she had no idea how to word a letter so as not to worry her mother even more than she was worried already.

'So you do think I'm shirking my duty!' Louise spoke into Emma's musings, and she turned from the rail to regard her critically.

'You know yourself you're not giving Jeremy the care which his parents expect you to do. You must have been much more proficient when they were at home?'

Louise merely shrugged her shoulders. It was plain her thoughts were elsewhere . . . on this evening and the excitement of dining with the man she had so foolishly fallen in love with.

'I didn't really know Paul then,' she submitted at last and then asked Emma if she were contemplating doing any sight-seeing while she was in Mauritius.

'I'd hoped to do some, yes, but as you are working I'll have to go on my own, which I'm not wildly excited about. . . .' She tailed off as Paul Fanchette came striding onto the lawn and glanced around, his face stern and set.

'He's looking for me,' from Louise self-deprecatingly. 'I ought to be with Jeremy.'

'I'd go if I were you,' recommended Emma. 'He doesn't appear to be in the best of moods.'

Louise, following her advice, went off and joined the little boy, and Paul went back into the house.

Emma's mood became pensive; she had recently admitted that it could have been extremely difficult for Louise not to fall in love with a man so attractive as Paul Fanchette, simply because she had always been far more impressionable than Emma; she was immature, easily influenced by people and by circumstances.

Pity welled up as Emma watched Louise moving with steps far more light and eager than before she received the invitation to dinner. Optimism seemed to ooze from her; she laughed when the ball hit her in the face and lifted a hand gaily to wave at Emma.

What reason had the wretched man for the invitation? There seemed no feasible explanation for it that Emma could see—unless, of course, he had begun to have pangs of guilt at not making Emma more welcome . . . Welcome? Why should he bother to make the sister of one of his employees welcome, anyway? His only interest seemed to be in her physical attributes!

Restless and depressed, Emma decided to take a swim, and a few moments later she was on the seashore, walking barefoot on the warm, soft sand, her towelling wrap open to reveal a pretty one-piece bathing costume.

She had been in the water for only a few minutes

when to her disgust Paul Fanchette came along, obviously with the same idea as she had had. She watched the long strides eat up the distance and realised he would enter the lagoon close to where she was swimming. She saw him toss his wrap and towel on the sand, then he was in the water, coming closer. . . .

Something akin to panic seizing her, she swam to the shore and picked up her wrap. Paul came ashore close behind her, reached for the wrap and took it from her trembling fingers.

What what was he up to now? she wondered, once again aware that she had placed herself in a vulnerable situation since there was not anyone else on this little curving beach which was, of course, the property of Paul.

'Give me my wrap!' she shot at him, having the greatest difficulty in not turning to run. His eyes were taking their fill of her figure from her shapely ankles to her thighs, her tiny waist, her breasts, so very plainly outlined beneath the wet costume.

'You have an exquisite form,' he murmured, eyes still lingering, an odd expression in their depths. 'Your sister tells me you are twenty-four years old. How is it you're still unmarried?'

'You asked Louise my age?' Emma looked at him in surprise, diverted for the moment and forgetting her need for her wrap.

'I was curious.' He flickered a glance to her face. 'I asked you a question. How is it that you're not married?'

'The reason should be obvious.'

'Nobody asked you?' in tones of mocking satire. He shook his head. 'I can scarcely believe that.'

'Perhaps the men I've met are all like you,' she could not resist retorting. 'They consider all women the same—fine to have an affair with but marriage—' She flipped a hand expressively. 'No fear! Far too risky!'

He threw back his head and laughed.

'I like your sense of humour, Emma.' He pointed to a spot at his feet. 'Come here,' he ordered, and now his voice was in a lower pitch, but unmistakably authoritative. Emma stayed where she was and again asked for her wrap. She was vitally aware of him as a man, the tensed muscles of legs and arms, the narrow waist and hips, the broad shoulders, powerful and straight. Lastly, the handsome face, bronzed and clear-skinned. Louise had said he was twenty-eight. He looked a couple of years older but no more than that.

Suddenly she was thinking of her mother who married a man fifteen years older than herself . . . and now she was widowed, and very lonely.

I'm only four years younger than Paul—with a gasp of disbelief Emma cut her thoughts. What on earth had brought a thing like that into her head!

'Emma . . .' Paul Fanchette's soft voice brought her eyes to his, and she saw the sternness in them, the glint of mastery. 'I told you to come here.'

'You ordered me to!'

'Have it how you wish.' A small, significant pause and then, 'Any order I give is usually obeyed.'

'Except this time! I'll have my wrap if you don't mind!' She was trying her best to appear cool and arrogant, but it was difficult when she was wearing such a scanty covering.

'If you don't obey me, Emma,' came the dangerously quiet words, 'I shall do something to you you'll not like at all.'

'You—!' The blood rushed into her face and she swiftly averted her eyes. 'You wouldn't dare!' she shot at him, almost dazed by the very fact of the threat. The man was too familiar by far!

'Wouldn't dare to spank you?' He spoke with amusement now, his whole manner having undergone a change. 'I rather think you'll be wise enough not to take the risk. For the last time, come here.'

Biting her lip with mortification, she nevertheless obeyed, something deep within her subconscious telling her that there was some specific reason for this man's attitude . . . but what could that reason be? The very fact of his order was an intimacy she would never have dreamed he'd show . . . and the threat he had made was even more intimate.

'That's better,' he said as she reached him. 'Now turn around.'

'What for?' So he could feast his eyes on her *other* curves! she supposed.

'I'm merely going to help you into your wrap,' was his amused reply. 'What a suspicious mind you have, Emma. Did you fear I was going to do something to embarrass you?'

She shot him a glowering look.

'Seeing that you've embarrassed me several times already, it would not be surprising if I expected the worst.' She had added the last word without thinking there might be a better one, and he laughed outright, showing strong, even, white teeth.

'The worst? Come, now, you enjoyed our little interludes of romance.'

Of torrid passion, more like! Naturally Emma did

not voice this correction. He held out the wrap, and she turned to put her arms in the sleeves.

'I do realise that repetition becomes boring, but I just have to say again that you're the most arrogant, pompous, self-opinionated man I have ever met!'

'Thanks,' casually as he turned her around again to fasten the belt of her wrap. The whole situation was ludicrous, she thought. Unreal, made so by the unpredictable character of the man. 'Your wording was a little different but the meaning was clear enough.' He had tied the belt, but his hand was in it so that she could not have moved away had she wanted to.

And with a shock of surprise that left her dazed, she was admitting that she did not want to move away. He smiled narrowly, eyes perceptive. 'Self-opinionated or not,' he commented smoothly, 'you are plainly asking me to kiss you—no, you don't, my girl!' he added when in anger she would have struggled for freedom. 'That temper of yours certainly needs to be curbed.' He bent to possess her lips, caressing moistly and with movements so sensuous that she felt she must reciprocate if he did not release her soon. This he did, slowly drawing his lips from her mouth to her cheek before drawing away from her altogether. He smiled faintly in amusement as he stared down into her lovely eyes, wide and limpid and somewhat shy. 'You'd have struggled away in your temper—if you could, that is. And immediately you'd have regretted it. You know very well, Emma, that you enjoy my kissing you equally as much as I enjoy doing it.'

True; she could not honestly deny it. She was

bewildered by what was happening to her; wondered if she were oversexed and had discovered it only now when this man with his ardour tempted her, for never before had she found herself drawn physically to any man. A kiss, yes, and an embrace. But never had she known the aching desire and excitement which Paul Fanchette could so easily arouse within her.

'I must go,' she said, and her voice was far from steady. Surely she wasn't following in her sister's footsteps and falling in love with the creature!

'I'm coming along, too,' he supplied as he picked up his own wrap. 'Did I tell you that dinner tonight will be at eight?'

'I knew it was; Louise told me you always dine at eight.'

'Louise. . . .' A frown touched his brow. 'Yes, she's coming too,' he added as if the recollection had just come to him.

Emma's nerves tensed. Louise had believed it was *she* whom Paul wanted . . . but Emma was now sure it was herself. Why? Of course! He was still hoping she would accept his offer of an affair—an affair that would result in her becoming richer than when she arrived here. Some imp of mischief prompted her to say, slanting him a provocative look, 'You mentioned wanting to have—an affair with me. Er—how long was it to be?'

The fine lips curved in a half smile.

'You told me to go to hell, remember? And now—are you considering my offer?' Something faded in his voice and suddenly his mouth was tight. The eyes glinted . . . at some secret thought? Or was he angry with her?

'I was simply curious to know how soon you would tire of me.'

He looked narrowly at her and said, 'What's the idea? Why the sudden interest in my proposal?'

'Oh, I'm not thinking of accepting,' she assured him, then frowned at what appeared to be a slackening of the taut facial muscles. This man certainly was a puzzle to her by these changes of expression. Emma wished she could understand him. 'I merely wanted to know how long you would have—er—found me attractive.'

'That,' he replied tersely, 'is something one cannot predict. However, as long as you reject my offer there seems no logical reason for discussing it, does there?' He was staring down into her face; she felt like a spanked child and consequently, subsided into silence. They were walking along the golden sands towards the small gate through which they would enter the chateau grounds. Before they reached it, Paul stopped, tilted her chin and said, 'You can begin calling me Paul, seeing that I have chosen to call you Emma.'

She coloured delicately, thinking of Louise and knowing she would be furious at this intimacy.

'I can't do that,' she stated firmly, 'nor do I want you to call me by my first name.'

'I already have and shall continue to do so.' He held her chin more tightly. 'You will do as I ask,' he told her, the warning light in his eyes matching the taut flexing of the jaw.

'But . . . Louise . . .'

'It has nothing to do with your sister. You know how I feel about her—'

'Then please feel the same way about me!' Emma

released herself, only to realise that her skin was still glowing from the warmth of his touch. She ought to get away. This dense emotion was in itself a warning, and she would be a fool not to heed it.

'Tonight at dinner I shall correct you if you dare address me as Monsieur Fanchette,' was his parting shot when presently they entered the hall of the house, each to go their separate ways.

Louise was giving Jeremy his tea when Emma went into the room set aside as a nursery.

"Hello!' he said with a bright smile. 'Will you read me a story when I get into bed?' His chubby face was bright and cheerful, his grey eyes sparkling. A charming little boy who didn't ask for much at all—and it was as well, was the grim thought which followed. For Louise gave him precious little and his uncle even less.

'Where have you been?' Louise wanted to know. 'You've been gone for well over an hour.'

'I went for a swim.'

'You did?' The blue eyes were curious. 'Paul went out there wearing a beach wrap. Did you see him—I mean, was he swimming at the same time as you?'

Emma nodded, said noncommittally, 'He was there, yes, but I came out. I never stay in for long as you know.'

'He spoke to you?'

Emma forced a little laugh and said,

'What is this—a cross-examination?' She turned to Jeremy. 'What story would you like? Pirates again?'

'Ooh, yes, please!'

Louise was eyeing her curiously, and she was bound to feel uncomfortable. She felt a sort of traitor, too, which was ridiculous since it was scarcely her fault if the man Louise loved was finding her sister attractive. Nevertheless, Emma knew a disloyalty in not being able to confide in Louise, but the whole situation was far too delicate. Emma wished she had never come here in the first place, for she had done no good at all. In fact, she could easily have done some harm, she mused grimly, for she could not see her sister being kept in ignorance for much longer, especially if, as he had threatened, Paul corrected her, Emma, should she use his surname. Well, there was at least a remedy for that: make sure she did not address him by any name at all.

Chapter Four

The sexy, citrus green dress was put aside in favour
of the blue, which though tight-fitting in the bodice,
was at least much higher in the neck. The skirt was
full, gathered into a nipped-in waistband through
which was threaded narrow, silver ribbon to meet in
the centre in a lover's knot. Ankle-length, it had a
regal quality about it and Louise immediately said
with a frown, 'Are you wearing that? I mean—it's
rather formal, isn't it, for dining at home?'

'Yours is formal too,' observed Emma, thinking
how lovely her sister looked in the long, peach-
coloured dress of frilled nylon and lace. The neckline was low-cut, and tiny frills formed the sleeves.

Louise wore a necklace and matching bracelet. The ear drops were made of shell, peach-coloured to match the dress. 'You look very glamorous,' she added with a smile.

'Do you think he'll notice?'

A small pause and then, 'Louise, try to forget him. He's not worth it, believe me. He's the kind of man who'll take advantage if you're not very careful.'

'Oh, and what do you mean by that?' Louise had come into Emma's room, and she stood watching as Emma put the finishing touches to her hair.

'He's a womaniser; I've already given you that as my opinion.'

'Has he made a pass at you, then?' Slow the words, with an edge of unmistakable animosity in their depths. Swiftly Emma shook her head, cursing Paul for making her lie like this.

'What a thing to ask! No, most certainly he hasn't made a pass at me!'

Louise walked over to the window and stood for a moment looking out in silence.

'Then why are you so sure he's a womaniser?' she inquired at length over her shoulder.

'It's obvious—'

'In what way?'

Emma swung round on the dressing stool.

'For heaven's sake, Louise, stop this questioning! The man's getting you down, and the sooner you make a firm decision to come home with me, the better it will be. Tell him—tomorrow, or even this evening—that you've decided to break the contract and leave. It'll give him plenty of time to find a replacement. But in any case, there are several housemaids here so he can get one of those to look after Jeremy.'

'I'm not leaving and that is that!'

Emma shrugged, used the perfume spray and suggested they go down to the salon where Paul had said they would drink aperitifs.

He was there when they entered, tall and immaculate in an oyster-coloured linen suit and pale mauve shirt lightly embroidered down the front. Not a hair out of place . . . and a pervasive smell of after-shave, or could be body lotion . . . obviously expensive, judging by the way it lingered. He stared unsmilingly at them in turn, his eyes narrowed and unfathomable. At this moment he seemed older, but in any case there was a certain maturity about him that could be attributed to a much older man, and certainly those threads of silver lent even further distinction, as did the tiny fan lines spreading out from the corners of his eyes. Emma hadn't noticed them until he laughed, although they were always there, faint but certainly discernible.

'Sit down,' he invited, spreading a hand. 'Emma, what would you like to drink?'

'Emma. . . .' The word formed on Louise's lips, and only Emma noticed it. She set her mouth, angry with Paul for using her given name. And she felt even worse on hearing him say after she had requested a dry sherry, 'And you, Miss Morris? What will you have?'

Louise was colouring up, and her small, white hands were clenched tightly in her lap. Emma shot Paul a furious glance, but he pretended not to see.

'I'll h-have a sherry too, b-but medium, please.' That she was fighting tears was plain, and Emma's heart went out to her. The man was callous—among all his other vices!

It was a bad beginning, but the meal proved to be a pleasant one, mainly because—surprisingly—Paul made sure that Louise was drawn into the conversation every time she went quiet, lost in her own unhappy thoughts.

The menu consisted of Creole dishes, mainly seafood. Emma found the lobster delicious, cooked in the Creole way, and for a dessert she had guava jelly with fresh fruit to follow, the large cut-glass bowl containing custard apples, litchis, slices of fresh pineapple and paw-paw, and small, pinkish bananas the flavour of which was different from the bananas to which she was used.

'It was a delicious meal,' she said in answer to Paul's inquiry as to how she had liked the Creole food.

'And you, Miss Morris?'

'Very tasty, thanks.' Louise managed a thin smile, but her eyes were dulled, her pretty mouth drooping.

Emma's eyes met Paul's across the table, and his lips quivered at the glowering look she gave him.

Coffee and liqueurs were served in the salon where they had earlier taken aperitifs, and as soon as she had finished, Louise rose from her deep armchair and said she was going to bed.

'So soon?' frowned Emma, sure she would succumb to a fit of weeping the moment she was in her room.

'I'm tired,' she returned briefly and walked to the door. 'Good night,' she said and went out.

For a long moment there was silence in the room. It was broken by Emma who said that she, too, was going to bed. She felt she must go to her sister even though she despaired of being of any practical help to Louise in her present frame of mind.

'You're going?' A heavy frown creased Paul Fanchette's brow. 'It's early—not yet half-past nine.'

She looked directly at him, mouth tight.

'You didn't say that to Louise, did you?'

He shrugged his broad shoulders.

'You know very well that I have no wish for her company.'

'But you wish for mine.' A statement, not a question, and it was accompanied by a glance of contempt not unmingled with deep censure. 'You're not going to gain anything, Monsieur Fanchette, by pursuing me like this. As for your attitude towards my sister—it's callous to say the least and, therefore, bound to antagonise me.'

'You appear to be devoted to your sister.'

'We've always been close—as a family—in fact. It hurts me to see her so unhappy.'

He became thoughtful, and his mood was neither the familiar mocking one nor the more severely serious one. He seemed softer in some indefinable way, and with a little shock, Emma found herself convinced that there was a third facet to the man's already complex personality.

'Are you trying to tell me that your sister is in love with me?' he said at last, a frown between his eyes.

Emma hesitated irresolutely, reluctant to give away Louise's secret. Yet almost immediately she was telling herself that it could do no real harm

. . . and it might just bring about a change of attitude in Paul: he might be willing to dismiss Louise as Emma wanted him to, sure that such an eventuality would be the girl's salvation. She could go home to the mother who loved her and forget all about her disastrous stay on the island of Mauritius.

'It's true, Monsieur Fanchette; Louise is in love with you—genuinely.'

A long silence ensued before he responded with, 'I doubt it, Emma. She strikes me as the kind who is looking to the main chance—'

'A gold digger!' resentfully and with a flaring of the temper which had never been so strongly in evidence as it had since she had come into contact with this hateful man. 'No such thing! Louise is a sweet girl, once you get to know her.'

'Sweet?' with a lift of his straight, black brows. 'A bore with her eye-play and continual thrusting her presence upon me.' He paused, his frown deepening. 'However, if as you say she's been stupid enough to—' He broke off impatiently, obviously unwilling to use the words: "fall in love" a second time. 'I'll agree to dismiss her,' he added at length. 'She can possibly return to England with you. . . .' Quite unexpectedly his voice trailed, and he was frowning more heavily than before.

Emma, with swift perception, said coldly, 'You don't want *me* to go, but as I've said, you'll gain nothing by pursuing me, for even were I to contemplate an affair you'd be the last man I'd choose.'

'You're frank,' he said, 'insultingly so.'

'Can it be that your ego is deflated at last?' Emma could not resist asking, and she saw his eyes narrow ominously.

'Be careful,' he recommended in a very soft voice. 'Don't carry the joke too far.'

Emma retorted recklessly, 'I've touched you on a raw spot and I'm glad. It was high time someone brought you down a peg.' She stopped somewhat abruptly on seeing him rise from his chair. He moved across the room with the swiftness and lithe grace of a jungle cat, giving Emma no time to escape. She was roughly jerked to her feet with such force that the breath was momentarily knocked out of her body.

'Let me go!' she blazed, twisting and writhing in her determination to avoid a repetition of what had happened twice already. Aware of his powerful magnetism and her own weakness, she fought with a strength she did not know she possessed. But against the sinewed strength of the man holding her, Emma's efforts were puny, and she was soon his captive, her body crushed against him, her lips possessed by his. They seemed to burn her flesh as they moved roughly, sensuously, exploring her temples, her throat, the delicate slope of her shoulder where, with his chin, he had managed to slip the neck of her dress to one side. He took her breast, gently kneading and squeezing, using his finesse to one purpose . . . that of making her eat her words of a few minutes ago when she had declared that he would be the last man with whom she would have an affair. He was resolved to bring her to surrender and although she knew this, she was powerless to do anything about it. For he was in command, and she the suppliant, her emotions heightened by the roving hands, the exploring mouth, the sinewed hardness of his long, lean body that was compelling her to arch hers to its shape and at the same time creating that now familiar desperate, unbearable ache of desire in her loins.

'Paul. . . .' She murmured his name huskily, her willing mouth parted and tempting. His eyes were burning embers of passion above her, and she felt that this time there would be no drawing back for either of them. Lifting her, he carried her to the couch and laid her down, then stood there staring at her face.

'Do you admit that you lied just now when you implied that you weren't drawn to me physically?'

She hesitated, would dearly have loved to deny she had spoken an untruth, but the desperate longing within her for fulfilment brought from her quivering lips the admission that she had in fact lied. The twisted smile of triumph was hateful to her, and she knew she ought to have the strength of will to rise up from where he had laid her, but she could not.

His voice was that of the victor as he said, 'So at last you are honest with yourself. There's nothing to be ashamed of in the natural desires of the flesh.' He paused a moment. 'You and I need each other, Emma. You must stay for a while and—' he stopped, frowning as he glanced at the door on which a timid knock had sounded. Emma hadn't heard it, but instinct prompted her to sit up, to straighten the neck of her dress and her skirt.

Paul shot her a glance as he said brusquely, 'Come in.'

Louise entered, eyes dull, lifeless. She looked from one to the other, bewildered in some way she could not understand.

'What is it?' demanded Paul shortly. 'Jeremy?'

She shook her head.

'I expect he's asleep. He never wakes once he does go to sleep.'

'Then what brings you back here?'

Emma moved uncomfortably, wondering if her sister guessed anything. She, Emma, had managed somehow to appear cool and collected—a miracle considering the tumult that was raging within her!

'I wanted to come back. I knew I'd not sleep, and as Emma was here I thought you wouldn't mind?' She looked up at him, lashes damp and stiff. 'You don't mind, do you?'

Paul was furious; Emma could see that and she said at once, 'As a matter of fact, Louise, I was just leaving. I'm very tired and am going to bed.' Rising from the couch, she turned, at the same time avoiding Paul's eyes. Nor did she look at him when she said, on reaching the door, 'Good night, Monsieur Fanchette.' She met her sister's gaze. 'You had better come with me,' she advised and deliberately took hold of her arm.

Paul said nothing, and Emma did wonder just what his thoughts were. Was he as frustrated as she? Of course, he must be. Yet even as she mounted the lovely balustraded staircase, Emma was owning to being relieved that she had been prevented from an act which she would almost immediately have regretted.

Once in Louise's bedroom she asked her why she had been crying.

'You know very well why. Oh, Emma, I'm so down I could kill myself!'

'Don't say such things, Louise!' Emma moved to put her arms about her shoulders. 'Think of Mother if nothing else. She's unhappy enough already. Look, you must leave—we both must! I insist—'

'Leave, and never see him again? I'd die—my heart's broken anyway—' Louise burst into a paroxysm of weeping, and try as she may Emma could not console her. She found herself cursing the man to whom she herself had almost surrendered. Yet was this misery which Louise was suffering entirely his fault? He could have been kinder, yes; but Emma rather thought that might have made things worse, as then Louise would naturally have surmised that there was some real hope for her.

'Try to compose yourself,' begged Emma, leading Louise to the bed and sitting her down. 'I can't leave you like this.'

'Go to bed, Emma. I shan't sleep anyway, so you won't do any good by staying. Oh, wasn't he horrid with me this evening? And why should he call you Emma and me—me b-by my surname? If he should get to like you, I really would kill myself, for I'd not be able to bear it!' She turned to bury her head in the pillow, and Emma found *herself* in tears. 'Please leave me,' beseeched Louise. 'I'm no fit company for anyone! Besides, I want to be on my own!'

'But you didn't want that just now when you came down to the salon,' Emma reminded her.

Louise sat up again and made some attempt to dry her eyes.

'If you must know, I hated the thought of your being alone with Paul.'

Silence reigned for a space, with Emma reliving that passionate interlude and thanking God that

Louise had thought to knock on the door and had not just walked in.

And in any case, what if she had come a minute sooner? It didn't bear thinking about, for the result would have been an irreparable rift between her and Louise, and perhaps between Emma and her mother.

'I do wish you could forget him—'

'That's a stupid thing to say and you know it! If you'd ever been in love, you'd know just how I feel! I've nothing to live for, Emma, nothing!'

Trying to comfort her was a futile and thankless task, and at last Emma listened to her sister's repeated pleas and left her alone.

But she did not go immediately to her room. She went down again to the salon. Paul was listening to classical music, played in low notes from a tape recorder. He glanced up, and she gave him a chill look in return.

'Louise is distressed—' That was an understatement if ever there was one! she thought. 'You meant it when you said you'd dismiss her, and we'd be able to go home together?'

He made no answer but merely set his jaw.

'You promised,' persisted Emma, 'and an honourable man would not go back on his word.'

'So you believe me to be an honourable man?' His tones were suave and low.

'I'm asking you to dismiss my sister from your service!'

'Come to me tomorrow sometime, and I'll give you my answer.'

So he was still hoping for an affair. She supposed he had every cause for optimism after what had happened less than an hour ago. His face was set, impassive; she knew it would be futile to argue with him and she turned to go.

He said softly, 'You do realise that your complete lack of embarrassment reveals much to me, don't you?'

She coloured faintly.

'I have admitted, I think, that—that you—draw me physically. But I shall not stay and be your mistress—'

'If your sister hadn't come in, I'd have had the promise from you.'

'A promise I'd have broken—yes—believe me,' she went on fiercely. 'I'd have regretted my—lapse within minutes.'

He shrugged impatiently.

'Go to bed, Emma. We're both tired. See me in the morning, and we'll have a long talk.'

The following morning there was a miraculous change in Louise.

'I was stupid last night,' she owned self-deprecatingly. 'Try to forget it, Emma. I feel much better this morning.'

Emma looked at her with a hint of suspicion.

'Are you sure?' she asked. 'You're not putting on an act?' Emma was a little frightened, for she could not easily forget her sister's threat of suicide.

'An act?' Louise's surprise was genuine, and Emma breathed a sigh of relief. 'No, of course not. I really do feel much better.'

'Then I'm glad.' A pause and then, 'I shall have to write Mother today. I've been putting it off, but I

can't do so any longer.' There was a question in the
words which Louise answered at once.

'Tell her I'm much happier.'

Emma said nothing. She felt extremely anxious
about Louise's reaction to her dismissal—
presupposing Paul kept to his word, that was. Emma
now had some cause for doubt, after his prevarica-
tion last night.

She went along to his study as soon as Louise had
taken Jeremy to school.

Paul was writing at his desk and did not at first
look up when, after knocking, Emma entered without waiting for an invitation. She glanced around,
noticing the tapestries along one wall, while two
other walls were lined with well-filled bookcases.
The wide, low window opened out to a verandah,
and the view was breathtaking—over the magnificent grounds of the chateau to the palm-fringed
beach and the sapphire blue lagoon. A graceful
white-sailed yacht was silhouetted against the azure
sky—Paul's yacht in which he took part in various
regattas.

She could picture him, dressed for the part, tall
and handsome and efficient. Did he ever take
women on a pleasure cruise? she wondered. Louise
did not seem to know much about him at all, but
then he had always kept her at a distance—or tried
to.

'You asked me to see you this morning,' she said,
moving from the door into the centre of the room.

'About my dismissing your sister, yes.' He was not
in the best of moods; in fact, he reminded her of the
stern, austere man she had first met, when he

seemed so rigidly formidable that she had wondered if he ever unbent.

Emma had certainly seen him unbend!

'It's important for everyone concerned.' Emma's voice was firm, decisive. 'You did promise,' she reminded him, and a frown appeared on his brow.

'I would have all the trouble of finding someone else,' he pointed out. 'Nannies are not easy to get, because the girls here can find jobs that give them more freedom. It was for that reason that Jeremy's parents advertised in the English papers.'

She looked at him across the desk. He had not stood up immediately on her entry, but he was rising now.

'You're going back on your promise, then?'

'Yes, I am.'

'And the real reason is because of me.' She waited but he made no comment. The frown was still creasing his brow. 'What good this attitude will do you I cannot fathom. I'm leaving at the end of the fortnight.'

'You said you might stay longer.'

'There isn't anything to stay for.' She moved restlessly, angry with him for breaking his promise.

'Given time,' he said with a growing frown, 'I could persuade you to stay.'

'Well, you don't happen to have the time,' was Emma's rather tart rejoinder.

His dark eyes met hers, fixed and deliberate.

'You know in your heart that you'd like to stay; you've admitted to being physically attracted to me, as I am to you, so why this attitude? Life is for living, Emma. I promised you'd be richer when you left—'
For some reason he cut abruptly and Emma sent him

an interrogating glance, waiting for him to continue. But he was now looking down at the leather-bound writing pad on which rested the paper he had been writing on when Emma entered the study. 'I'm busy, Emma, and have no more time to give you. The question of Louise is closed as far as I am concerned. However, if she herself does want to break the contract there is little I can do about it. I have, nevertheless, quite categorically refused to release her, so she will not be given a testimonial if she does decide to leave.'

Emma sighed deeply.

'You're fairly confident that she won't leave of her own accord, aren't you?'

'Emma,' he said with some asperity, 'I have told you I'm busy. Please leave—and this time, kindly close the door behind you.'

Chapter Five

The next few days passed far more pleasantly than those that had gone before. Louise seemed to be making a determined effort to pull herself together, and in consequence she was more like her old self. Emma wrote to their mother and hoped she had eased her mind a little. Louise also attended more conscientiously to her small charge, but Paul also gave him a little of his time, and on one occasion Emma joined them in a game of hide-go-seek in the spacious grounds of the chateau.

On another occasion Paul asked Emma if she was intending seeing a few interesting places and to her surprise said that Louise could have a couple of days off in order to show her around. One of the Creole maids, Sarogni, would look after Jeremy when he came from school.

'It's good of Paul to let me off, isn't it?' Louise and Emma were ready to go out, both looking lovely in bright cotton frocks and sandals. Emma had managed to acquire a honey-tan which added to her attractiveness, and Paul, coming upon them as they came from the chateau, halted for a moment; and his eyes were flickering over her from head to foot. And if Louise noticed that he gave her far less attention, she made no comment when once again she and Emma were alone, walking now towards where the small car was parked. The use of this had been Louise's only for taking Jeremy to school and bringing him home again. But another concession made by Paul was that the two girls could have the car for sightseeing, and in fact, any time they wanted to go out in the evening.

'I'm a little mystified by the change in Paul.' Louise voiced her thoughts after starting up the car and driving it to the high, wrought-iron gates which terminated the long, wide avenue of flame trees which were an especial feature of the chateau grounds. 'I never expected him to let us have the car.'

'It was good of him,' was all Emma returned to this. She knew that Paul was doing it for her sake, having realised that she had seen little outside the grounds of the chateau and the private beach curving to the south of it. He had not mentioned anything more about an 'affair,' and she wondered if he had forgotten all about it. His manner was mostly indifferent; he had not invited the girls to dinner after that one occasion.

'We'll go to Port Louis first,' Louise had said earlier, and now she was driving towards it, having been there several times with Mrs. Winnick who, Emma gathered, was a charming woman, far more human than her brother.

Soon after entering the sunlit city, Louise parked the car, and the first place she took Emma to was the palm-lined Place d'Armes, which was off the lovely main square and where Emma enjoyed sitting in a garden cafe and admiring the French colonial buildings erected in the eighteenth century.

'I didn't realise how very French Mauritius is,' she remarked after having noticed some of the street names.

'Neither did I before I came. The French claimed the island early in the eighteenth century and called it the Ile de France, and it became a prosperous French colony, so the language, customs and religion are still here, although English is the official language. It's attractive, isn't it—being so French, I mean?'

Emma nodded her head.

'Yes, I love it.'

'Could you live here?'

A pause. She wondered what Louise would have to say were she to tell her she could live here . . . as Paul's mistress.

'I guess it would be a very wonderful place to live—but not possible for me, so I shall have to be content with having another holiday sometime.'

'I was thrilled when I first came. The Winnicks were super people, so kind to me. Mrs. Winnick used to take me with her quite often when she went shopping. They both treated me more like one of the family, and I always ate in the evenings with them.'

'So it was very different when you went to the chateau of her brother.'

'Yes, very different indeed. I suppose I was unhappy right from the start. I felt strange in Paul's home. . . .' She tailed off, and watching her expression, Emma knew just where her thoughts were.

'You fell for Paul's good looks and that made things much worse.'

Louise nodded in agreement.

'And I now realise, Emma, that I—well—began to push myself—' She broke off, colour tinting her cheeks. 'He hated being—how can I put it?' Again she paused but then said deprecatingly but with perfect frankness, 'Chased is the only word to describe how it was; I fully realise it now. And a man as arrogant and superior as Paul was bound to give me the brush-off, wasn't he?'

Emma was at a loss to find a response, for she had not expected Louise to open up like this and admit to having annoyed Paul—for that was undoubtedly what her conduct amounted to.

'You seem to be getting over it,' submitted Emma tentatively.

'I'm trying hard,' agreed her sister, managing to produce a smile. 'Unrequited love is fruitless, and the sooner I can forget him the more comfortable life will be.' Her lip trembled, but she soon pulled herself together.

Emma said gently, 'Come home with me, Louise. Mother will be so glad to have you back.'

Louise nodded thoughtfully, while Emma held her breath.

'It would be the wisest course, wouldn't it?'

'Under the circumstances, yes, Louise, it would.'

'It'll mean breaking the contract.'

'So . . . what does it matter? If the Winnicks were coming back shortly, it would be different, but you say they're not due back for almost two years?'

'That's right. I know they'll expect me to stay on until they return.' A sigh escaped her, and for a while the two sipped their coffee in silence. 'They were so good to me,' she murmured at length, almost to herself. 'It's not very nice of me to leave.'

'In this particular case you have to think of yourself first,' Emma pointed out practically. 'I'm sure that if Mrs. Winnick were in possession of the facts, she would agree.'

'Yes, I'm sure she would. But as she doesn't know the facts, she's going to think it was a dirty trick on my part to leave Jeremy.'

'Nevertheless, you are leaving?' Emma held her breath again, then let it out slowly and thankfully on hearing Louise say, 'I am leaving, yes, Emma. I realise just how stupid I've been.' She looked at her sister. 'Had it been you, you'd have been stronger, wouldn't you? You'd never have fallen victim to Paul's good looks and other perfections.'

Naturally Emma had nothing to say to this! For she had come closer by far to falling victim! She had almost given herself to the man.

'Shall we move on?' Louise opened her handbag and took out sunglasses. 'I shall miss this lovely sun,' she sighed as she put them on.

'But you'll be happier in yourself. Oh, Louise, I'm so glad you're coming home with me! Mother will be thrilled, too. She's missed you, Louise.'

'It troubled me,' she admitted. 'Yes, I shall be doing the right thing all round by coming home with you.' She paused while Emma paid the waitress, a lovely Creole girl with the name: Vivoosee, pinned to her royal blue apron. 'I don't know how I am going to give Paul my notice,' she added with a visible shudder when the girl had gone. 'However, I'll manage it somehow.'

Emma was silent, thinking about Paul and knowing he would be furious at this turn of events; he'd blame her she felt sure—and, of course, he would have cause to do so since it was by her persuasion that Louise was leaving the island. What of the little boy? Emma felt sorry for him but supposed that, adaptable as he seemed to be, he would soon get used to the new nanny his uncle would procure for him.

They went to the harbour, one of the finest in the Indian Ocean, first named Turtle Bay—Rade des Molluques—by the Dutch, but Port Louis was later created by the famous soldier and sailor, Mahe de Labourdonnais who became Governor of the island, changing it from a mere trading post to what it was today. Numerous ships and boats of all shapes and sizes lay at anchor in the magnificent bay. From there Louise took Emma to the market—a fantastic conglomeration of noisy people and multicoloured fruits and vegetables. One could hardly walk between the stacks of produce or crowds of shoppers and stall owners.

'It's incredible!' exclaimed Emma. 'Fascinating.' She was thoroughly enjoying the outing, partly, she supposed, because Louise was like her old self, a good companion and friend. Partly, though, because of the uniqueness of her surroundings. It was hard to imagine that once upon a time almost the entire island had been covered with thick forests of ebony trees, mainly Dutch red ebony—tambalacoque, tatamaka and others. Most had been cut down for sugar and tea plantations such as were owned by Paul Fanchette.

'Shall we drive on now to Curepipe?' suggested Louise after they had seen more of the city and had taken lunch at a restaurant called La Flore Mauricienne where they ate squid in Creole sauce served with saffron rice. For dessert they had fresh fruit and little coconut biscuits.

'Yes, whatever you say,' answered Emma. 'I'm really enjoying myself.'

'At last,' briefly but with meaning.

'It's such a relief—'

'I'm not myself yet,' broke in Louise warningly. 'You have no idea the difficulty I have in not bursting into tears.'

Emma swallowed, having been aware, of course, that Louise was by no means recovered yet. That was impossible, but at least some progress was being made.

Curepipe was the chief residential town of the island, with interesting shops where Emma bought her mother a Chinese ivory carving and some hand-embroidered handkerchiefs. From Curepipe they drove to the Machabee Forests where a guide showed them trees a thousand years old; later they stopped at the Plaine Champagne, parking the car and taking the five minutes' walk to get a spectacular view of the Rivière Noire gorges where all was silent, motionless—except for the roar of the water-falls. No other sound or movement.

'It's eerie,' said Louise, but Emma did not find it so. Finally they stopped for afternoon tea at a cafe on a glorious, palm-studded beach where the lagoon looked like blue glass, without a ripple as it touched the shore.

'It's been a lovely day out.' Contentedly Emma leant back in her seat, while Louise drove back to the chateau, passing a sugar factory and miles of estates with many white villas for the employees. An Indian temple came as a surprise, but it was the flowers that often caught and held Emma's atten-tion—the flaring hibiscus, crimson, rich pink, orange. The delicate allamandas, the lovely flame trees and numerous others, all lending flamboyant colour and shape and scent.

It was half-past seven when they arrived back. Dinner was served to them by Kamal, a tall, Creole manservant with a broad smile and dark, happy eyes.

'We are to have company,' he said by way of casual conversation as he laid down the large tray on which was far more than the girls needed—chicken and lamb, both served with rice, and pastries to follow.

'Company?' echoed Louise. 'You mean, someone is coming to stay here?'

He nodded his head.

'Monsieur's mother and brother, and, I believe, a distant cousin. They are coming for a week.' He bowed and went out.

'You never mentioned any relatives.' Emma now wondered why she should have assumed Paul to have only the one relative, his sister who was in Sri Lanka.

'Oh, didn't I? Mrs. Winnick mentioned them. He has another sister besides Mrs. Winnick, that is, and a brother. His mother lives in the Seychelles and comes over about once every six months, but she didn't come while I was with the Winnicks.'

'A week. . . .' Emma looked at her sister, watching her serve the meats onto the plates. 'I'm sure I shall feel in the way.'

'This house is large enough.'

'Yes. In any case, you and I shan't be invited to meet these people.'

But Emma was mistaken. Paul made a point of introducing Emma to his mother, a woman of elegance and charm, with immaculate blue-grey hair and a clear, dark skin. She seemed interested to know why Emma was here, and so it seemed that Paul hadn't bothered to explain anything.

'So you're Louise's sister? It'll be nice for her to have you here. How long are you staying?'

'About another week, I think.'

'And how long have you already had?' They were in the salon; it was three days since the outing, and two, since Louise had taken Emma up to spend the entire day on the most glorious beach on the island, far north, and a little south of Cap Malheureux. Louise was now back on duty, and at this moment on her way to bring Jeremy from school.

'A week,' answered Emma, and Madame Fanchette frowned.

'So you'll have had only two weeks! It's not long enough, my dear.' She spoke with an accent; earlier Emma had heard her talking in French to her son. She looked at Paul now, standing with his back to the window, watching the two women talking, a curious expression on his face. 'Can't you persuade her to stay longer, Paul? I'm sure you agree that two weeks is not long enough.'

'I've already exerted my persuasive powers,' was his urbane rejoinder, 'but to no avail. Emma is determined to go home at the end of the fortnight.' The dark eyes held a metallic glint, and Emma lowered her lashes. Undoubtedly he still wanted her to stay, despite his mood of near indifference during the last few days.

'You won't stay?' Madame Fanchette lifted an eyebrow in surprise. 'Is there some pressing reason why you cannot stay longer? It's such a way to come, just for two weeks.'

'I can't stay longer; it's not possible.' She could in fact stay on for another week but now, more than ever, she wanted to get away, just in case Louise should begin having second thoughts about going home.

The other two relatives were in their rooms, unpacking, and although Emma would have liked to get away, at the same time she was curious about the brother, wondering if he were in any way like Paul. And the cousin—what was he like?

The brother arrived in the salon and was introduced. A charming, young man about five years younger than Paul, he had a handsome face and a swift, spontaneous smile, but he in no way resembled his brother as regards arrogance and poise. Of course, the difference in ages would have a great deal to do with that, decided Emma who took an instant liking to the man, vitally aware as she chatted with him that Paul's eyes were on her, boring into her profile.

The third visitor came just as afternoon tea was being served, and Emma gave a start of surprise on seeing that the cousin was a girl. Why she should have surmised it was a man she could not have said. The girl was English, tall and blonde with a slender, supple figure and the self-assurance of a beauty queen. She had come from England to spend a year with Madame Fanchette, being distantly related to her through Madame Fanchette's grandmother, who was English. Obviously she and Paul had met before . . . in fact, Emma, watching them together, had a strong suspicion that they had at one time been very good friends. There was a certain familiarity in the way they talked, with heads bent towards each other, and in the way she picked up the silver teapot immediately Paul's cup was empty.

And she helped him to sugar . . . one teaspoonful. . . .

'You and Louise will join us for dinner,' said Paul smoothly when at last Emma rose to go.

'Oh—er—'

'At half-past eight, but in here at eight for drinks.' His dark eyes fixed hers, challengingly. She coloured and swung away swiftly.

'Very well,' she returned and with a rather muffled 'excuse me,' she reached the door and went out.

*   *   *

'We're to have dinner with them?' frowned Louise who had not yet been introduced to any of the visitors. 'Emma, how am I to tell Paul I'm leaving?'

'If I were you I'd do it now, at once. He's in his study; I saw him go in about ten minutes ago.'

Louise shook her head.

'It would make things awkward for this evening.'

A sigh escaped her sister.

'I wish he hadn't invited us.'

'So do I, in a way, but on the other hand I shall be interested to see what his mother is like.'

'Charming, and so is his brother. I can't make up my mind about the girl. She seems—well—possessive in her manner with Paul.'

'Possessive?' shortly and with keen interest. 'Are they—friends?'

'I gained that impression.'

'Good friends?'

Emma nodded reflectively.

'She seemed familiar—knew how much sugar he took—not that that means anything. However, I did get the idea that they'd been rather more than friends. . . .' She stopped, aware an access of dejection creeping into her mind. 'I've said he's a womaniser, so it could be that this Eileen is an old flame of his—*one* of them.'

'I see. . . .' Louise became thoughtful. 'Perhaps I shall see Paul at once. It will get the wretched business off my mind.'

'You don't seem too troubled about this girl.'

'You expected me to be jealous? Do you know, Emma, my whole attitude regarding Paul has changed. I still think he's something very special, but he's not the one for me. He's dictatorial, superior—not warm and tender the way I would want my husband to be. It seems that once I'd determined to clear my mind and look at things logically, I began to see the faults in him. I feel sure now that it was only a crush and not real love at all. With the passing of each day I'm forgetting I ever cared about him. In fact, I know for sure now that I wouldn't have him if he wanted me.'

Emma had been listening wide-eyed. She herself had at first believed it to be a crush, but later Louise had convinced her that she was in love with Paul. Well, it was a relief to know that Louise wouldn't be breaking her heart when she left and taking months to recover.

'I'm so glad,' breathed Emma with a smile. 'You had me really worried, Louise, and you certainly did seem to be shattered by your feelings for him.'

'I know, and I feel so ashamed at saying I wanted to die.'

Emma could laugh now.

'Go along, love, and get it over with. Tell him you're coming home with me next Saturday.'

'He'll be furious.' Louise seemed to have lost the courage she'd had a few moments ago. 'He makes me tremble when he looks at me with that particular glint in his eyes and sets his mouth.' She bit her lip, paused a moment and then, looking at her sister, 'You wouldn't—er—do it for me, would you, Emma?'

'You really want me to?' Emma was by no means averse to the task since it would afford her exceptional satisfaction to tell Paul she was taking Louise with her.

'If you would—I know it's asking a lot, and he'll most likely frighten you as well—'

'Stop worrying,' broke in Emma to reassure her. 'I'll manage him all right.'

'Thanks,' gratefully and with a drawn breath of relief. 'You're a brick, Emma. I'm so glad my parents adopted you.'

A smile lit Emma's lovely eyes.

'So am I,' she returned and went along to Paul's study.

He glanced up as she entered after knocking once.

'Can you give me a few minutes?' she asked and moved further into the room.

Paul's eyes swept over her entire figure.

'It seems I have no option,' was his dry rejoinder. 'What is it? If it'll take long then have a chair.'

'Thank you.' Although she sat down, she said at once, 'I've come to tell you that Louise is coming home with me next Saturday.'

A silence followed, intense, electrically charged as if a fire was about to break out.

'This is your doing, of course.'

'I did try to persuade her, yes, but it so happens that she herself made the decision.'

'Well, she would have to, wouldn't she?' Again the smooth, fine-toned voice was dry.

Emma coloured up.

'I don't think there is any more to say; so I'll go—'

'In a moment!' Imperious the tone and the flip of a hand which was an order for her to sit down again even though she had only half risen from the chair anyway. 'You do realise that I am entitled to at least one month's notice?'

'Well, you can't have it,' Emma told him shortly. 'Louise is breaking her contract, so the question of notice is not all that important.'

'I am supposed to find another nanny in a week?'

'Sarogni is very good with Jeremy. She'll take good care of him until you find a replacement for my sister.'

He looked at her hard and long, his jaw flexed, mouth tight.

'Why didn't Louise come herself?'

'If you want the truth: you frighten her.'

At this a twist of amusement affected the firm line of his mouth.

'But I don't frighten you, apparently?'

She looked at him, even now vitally affected by his powerful male magnetism, his mastery and commanding personality.

'I'm not afraid of you, no,' she stated at last.

'Not at this moment, and in these particular circumstances,' he agreed slowly, 'but in other circumstances . . . what then, Emma? I can put fear into you, can't I? Fear of both yourself and me.'

Her colour heightened; she stood up, not really surprised to find her legs were weak.

'I've said what I came to say, so I'll go.' She stopped a moment then added, 'Do you still want us to dine with you and your family?'

'Of course. Why ask?' That he was suppressing anger was plain. He had failed, both in keeping Louise and Emma herself. And failure was not a thing to which he was used.

'I naturally thought you'd be so annoyed that you'd prefer us not to dine with you.'

'I know you believe I have many faults,' he began, 'and you are probably right. However, one of my faults is not pettiness.' His voice was almost harsh, and censure edged the words. 'I did admit that should your sister decide to leave, I could do nothing about it.' He paused frowningly. 'I felt so sure she would not leave,' he murmured thoughtfully. 'Some change has come about apparently?'

Emma hesitated, but not for long.

'She no longer cares anything about you,' she informed him and at the same time watching closely for any change of expression, but his face was a mask.

'I'm glad,' was all he said, and the note of finality in his voice was quite sufficient for Emma to take the hint and make an immediate departure.

Chapter Six

'What are you wearing?' Louise asked when, after putting Jeremy to bed and Emma had read until he fell asleep, the two girls were having a quiet few moments in Louise's little sitting-room.

'I don't know.' She thought of the sexy, citrus green dress but felt it would not be quite the thing. She was thinking of Paul's mother; she did not want to shock her . . . or was it that she did not wish to give a wrong impression?

'You have that lovely pan velvet skirt with the gold trimming on the pockets and hem,' Louise reminded her. 'Your white blouse would go with it—you did bring that pretty evening one with the high collar that ties at the back?'

'Yes, I brought that one. I think I agree with you that the two together would make an attractive outfit.'

'The skirt's long and full—it falls so softly in folds that widen out from the waist.'

'What are you wearing?' Emma wanted to know once her own needs had been catered for.

'A dress you haven't seen because I bought it here, at the boutique in Curepipe where Mrs. Winnick used to go. It's a sort of midnight blue and the material's a bit like taffeta. It's stiff, and the skirt's fairly full so it sticks out. I like it and so did Mrs. Winnick. It has a fairly low neckline and small puff sleeves.' She had still not met the three visitors, but Emma had described them all to her. 'This girl you mentioned—I expect, from the sound of her, that she'll be dressed up to the nines.'

'I agree if the clothes she was wearing at teatime were anything to go by. She certainly has money. I'd make a guess that what she had on came originally from Paris.'

'Well, you and I must take particular care—not to compete, of course,' she added with a wry grimace, 'but to hold our own if possible.'

There was still half an hour or so before it was time to dress, and as Louise suddenly decided to wash her hair which, being very short and not very thick, would easily be dried in time, Emma decided on a stroll in the gardens. She loved the neat and spacious grounds of the chateau and had discovered several shady and secluded places where she could sit quietly and know there was little chance of her being disturbed. It was to one of these that she found herself proceeding and on reaching it she sat down on the little, rustic seat and relaxed. She was far happier than she was a few days ago when Louise was so distressed. But despite her satisfaction at the idea of getting away in less than a week's time, Emma was conscious of a weight pressing on her like lead. No use pretending she did not know the cause. Paul's handsome face seemed always to be before her mental vision, and his magnetism drew her so that there were times when, like her sister, she could have sought him out on some pretext or other, just to be near him.

Was it love?

You didn't fall in love with a man like that! His undisguised contempt of women was more than enough to put any of that sex off . . . or was it?

Some men possessed that certain something which was irresistible; hence, the good times they had in consequence, strewing broken hearts along the way with about as much concern as if they were watching petals falling from a tree.

Louise had been drawn to him, but what she felt turned out to be nothing more than a crush. Emma knew that what she herself felt was something rather more deep than that . . . though just how deep she was not inclined to discover.

Of one thing she was sure: the sooner she left the Chateau Fanchette and its owner, the better.

She had been sitting there, lost in reverie, for about five minutes when she became aware of voices drifting to her from somewhere behind the little arbour. Paul and his mother, and they seemed to be standing still, as if they had paused in their stroll.

'Don't you think she is more beautiful than ever, Paul?'

'Without a doubt she is.' There was a noticeable lack of expression in Paul's voice, as if he would hide his feelings from his mother.

'I think you should be considering marriage soon. . . .' She changed to French, but Emma could get the gist of what she was saying. 'This philandering's been going on quite long enough. Besides, I would dearly love to have grandchildren around me before I get too old to have patience with little ones.'

Paul laughed, and Emma could easily imagine his attractiveness, for she herself had caught her breath whenever he had laughed.

'Rita is the one you have to blame, my dear. She effectively illustrated just what women are—'

'Women?'

'Present company excepted,' he laughed. 'You know what I mean.'

'You loved her rather too well, my son. It is dangerous to love as deeply as that. Yet . . . what am I saying? It is possible to be loved as deeply, and then you are both lucky. But you—you left yourself open to hurt—'

'Shall we not discuss it, Mother,' broke in Paul somewhat crisply. 'It all happened five years ago, and as far as I am concerned it's forgotten.'

'But its effects remain; you're a philanderer with no respect for women. You suspect them all of an ulterior motive if they show the slightest interest in you.' There was a small pause; Emma felt she should move away, but if she did so now, she was bound to be seen, and she would rather not have those two know she had overheard their conversation about a girl called Rita whom Paul had once loved . . . too deeply. 'All women are not gold diggers, dear. Eileen's a sweet girl who'll make you a good wife. You did care for her once—not so long ago, in fact, and I had high hopes of a marriage. What happened? Eileen won't tell me, so now I'm asking you?'

'I was never serious with her. Oh, I agree she has all it takes to be the wife of a businessman who has at times to entertain, but—'

'Then why not consider it?' his mother broke in.

'Consider what?'

'Don't be obtuse!' The woman's tones were cool and edgy now. 'Marriage—you know very well what I mean!'

Paul was quiet for a space and then he laughed.

'I appreciate your concern, Mother, but I am quite happy with my bachelor life. Freedom is precious, and one would be a fool to give it up . . . especially when women are so cheap.'

'I am exasperated with you, my son! You haven't told me what happened between you and Rita.'

'I said we'd not discuss Rita. However, if it will assuage your curiosity, I shall tell you. Rita, while engaged to me, went off for a week-end with an ex-fiancé. Until then I had no idea she had been engaged before; she never thought to tell me.' Paul's tones were bitter. 'Are you now satisfied that I had reason to throw her over?'

'I didn't realise. . . . All I knew was that the break caused you much pain, but I believed it was *she* who'd jilted *you*.' There was a long silence, and Emma began to think they had walked on, but just as she was about to rise she again heard Madame Fanchette's voice. 'You were very young, though— too young, perhaps. The experience has made you bitter and wary. And it has turned you into a womaniser of the worst kind.'

'There is only one kind of womaniser,' argued Paul with a laugh, 'the kind that likes to take women to bed, who likes variety—'

'Stop it! I dislike you intensely when you talk like this! I've brought Eileen with me on purpose—'

'I gathered that, Mother.' Paul's voice was dry.

'I'm not matchmaking, Paul, but I do want you to bring this nonsense to a stop! Eileen's a charming girl who cares for you, so do please me by being nice to her.'

'I have no intention of being otherwise.'

'But . . . she's no appeal . . . ?'

'Not in that way.' A little pause and then, 'Mother, I am no different from any other man when it comes to being—chased, for want of another word. If ever I do marry, it'll be to a woman who lets *me* chase *her*.'

'You put it crudely, but I do understand what you mean. However, my son, with your looks, and all the rest that Nature gave you, women will always run after you.'

'Can we change the subject?' said Paul a little stiffly, and it was his mother's turn to laugh.

'You never did like my remarking on your—'

'If having grandchildren is so important to you,' broke in Paul shortly, 'then why not confine your efforts to Pierre?'

'He's young; you are almost twenty-nine.'

'I think,' said Paul abruptly changing the subject,

'that we ought to be getting back to the house. It's a quarter past seven.'

Emma waited until she heard the voices become indistinct before getting up from her seat, her expression pensive as she went over what she had heard.

Paul deeply in love . . . that was certainly an eye-opener, for she had branded him hard, unable to feel deeply for anyone. And he'd been let down, hence, his attitude towards women. The fact of their running after him had undoubtedly helped in his general estimation of their character. He was satisfied with his bachelor existence, but if ever he did marry, it would be to a woman who did *not* run after him, a woman whom he could woo in the old-fashioned way, it would seem. Yes, Emma had certainly discovered traits which she had never for a moment believed he could possess. She had thought he was ever conscious of his looks, his attraction for women, but underneath that debonair and egotistical self-assurance there was a modesty which to Emma was very appealing. It would be a lucky woman who eventually won him for a husband—if ever any woman did succeed in doing so, that was.

Walking slowly back to the chateau, Emma continued to dwell on what she had overheard and what conclusions she had come to as a result. She smiled to herself: never would she have believed that she'd have considered Paul's wife as lucky!

But she *had* decided that, once he was married, Paul would be the faithful kind; she reflected and realised that her thoughts were becoming rather muddled.

'Drat the man!' she exclaimed. 'What makes him

so complex? And why should I concern myself anyway!'

The dining salon was illuminated with candles only, and the effect was both cosy and romantic. Madame Fanchette was dressed in a Paris creation of three-quarter length dress made of a soft, nylon-like material embellished with silver threads running through it. The colour was aquamarine—no, decided Emma, rather more blue than that, because it brought out the blue-grey of her perfectly coiffured hair. Eileen wore a sleek, ankle-length dress of satin, embroidered with silk of several bright colours. There was a Chinese style about it in the slits which reached the girl's thighs and the high mandarin collar.

When Emma had entered the sitting-room, or main living salon as Louise called it, Paul's eyes had immediately flickered to her in a brief but all-examining look which took in her whole appearance, from her gleaming, well-brushed hair, to her face and throat, lower to her curves and finally to her feet, clad in dainty, strapped sandals with high, slender heels.

She saw him swallow before quickly asking her what she would like to drink. He had turned away after serving her, giving his whole attention to Eileen.

At the dinner table he sat next to her—she was on his left, his mother on his right. Emma was next to Louise, and Pierre sat opposite to them. He was chatty, charming to be with, and Louise, in particular, seemed to be getting along splendidly with him. Afterwards, back in the main salon with its deep

armchairs and soft carpet, Pierre sat close to Louise,
and Madame Fanchette chose to sit beside Emma on
the couch. This left Paul and Eileen together, a little
apart from the others, because the couch on which
they were sitting was at the far end of the room.
Conversation flowed between them all at times while
at others there was a temporary pairing off, and it
was then that Emma gave her attention to the
handsome couple—Paul and the girl his mother
would like him to marry. A weight settled on
Emma's stomach and she wondered why. Or did
she . . . ? No use denying that she wished it was her
to whom he was giving his attention.

Often, though, Emma found his eyes on her, his
expression inexplicably embarrassing. It was so intense, she realised, and that made her uncomfortable.

Madame Fanchette was the first to leave; she was
tired, she said, and bade them all good night. Louise
and Pierre were in close conversation, and often
Emma heard them laughing together. She herself
began to feel restless, and the weight of dejection
seemed to have spread itself evenly over her whole
body. She felt left out, which was both humiliating
and uncomfortable, but to get up and leave seemed
a reluctant course, because it would draw everyone's
attention to her; and there would follow that awkward few moments while she made her way to the
door and went out.

However, she decided on that course, and rising,
she said quietly, embracing them all, 'Good night;
I'm for bed too.' Her eyes met the swift glance of
Paul, who had been conversing in what could only be

described as an intimate way with Eileen. The girl also sent Emma a glance, one of indifference, and she was quickly giving her attention to Paul again without even responding to Emma's words.

'Going so early?' from Paul, and Emma shrugged carelessly and said yes, she was tired.

He rose to open the door for her; their eyes met again, to hold this time before Emma fluttered her lashes down, little knowing just how attractive the resulting shadows were as they fell on cheeks that were rather paler than usual. Somehow, their hands touched as she passed through the door and a tremor went through her.

'Sleep well,' he said softly, but she made no answer, for her throat was too dry for speech. She turned in silence and heard the door close quietly behind her.

In her room she undressed, then showered, because she knew that if she went to bed she would not sleep. After towelling she picked up a nightdress, held it for a while and heaved a deep sigh. Why go to bed when she was so restless, so confused in mind that she would only lie there wide awake?

On sudden impulse she donned a pair of slacks and a light sweater and went downstairs again and out to the garden. All was quiet but for the occasional call of a night bird or other creature. The moon was almost full, painting the landscape with an argent hue, while in the near distance the lagoon was a sheet of silver, smooth for the most part but beaten here and there as the ripple of a breeze passed over it. The reef sparkled with a million points of silver, and way beyond, the endless sea was dark. She walked along now familiar pathways, stopping occasionally to admire in the moonlight what she had admired in the sunshine—a mango on the edge of an orchard, with an exotic creeper clinging to it, purple blossoms clustered and dangling like fuchsias; a meranti tree and a hedge of pink and white oleanders, a juniper tree. . . .

She would miss it all so much! In spite of everything she felt at home here, especially in the gardens from where she could gaze out to the exquisite beauty of a palm-fringed shore, where she could stand and listen to the zephyr of a breeze soughing through the casuarinas, or wander to the less formal places to appreciate the tapestry of colour woven by a myriad of wild flowers whose heady perfume filled the air around her. Earlier the sky had been sapphire blue dotted with fine white, cirrus clouds, golden-lined. Now it was purple, star-spangled.

She wandered on, half inclined to walk along the shore, but before she could make up her mind she knew a tingling of nerves, a warning she was not alone out here, and she swung around in a full circle.

Paul . . .

He saw her shadowed figure against the grenadilla hedge through which argent light was slanting, and he came slowly towards her, steps long and light, head erect, set proudly on broad, arrogant shoulders. Quivers, nerves, racing heartbeats . . . once again she was alone with him in an isolated spot. . . .

'I thought you said you were tired?' Reaching her, he spoke softly and with a dry challenge. 'Wanted to get away . . . from me?'

'I—suppose so—' Not a tactful admission, but she

could think of nothing else to say on the spur of the moment.

'I have always liked your honesty.' His tones were stiff, unemotional.

'I'm sorry—I wasn't thinking.' She edged away, because he was too close; she could smell the lingering perfume of body lotion, and mingling with it, the almost intoxicating male odour of him. What was wrong with her to be affected like this! Desperate not to let him guess at her feelings, she found herself saying rather coldly, 'I'm going in now; please allow me to pass.'

Paul stood where he was, blocking her path.

'You were going in that direction,' he reminded her. 'Were you intending to walk along the beach?'

She coloured in the moonlight. She should have known it would gain her nothing to lie to him. She glanced towards the shore, where a little way out, Paul's yacht was moored to a jetty, the white sails bending in the breeze, and above it and the sea, the endless canopy of the sky, filled with stars . . . billions of them, spreading away into eternity. Emma felt small and insignificant, lost somehow, and wanting reassurance and comfort. The cosmos was too vast; it frightened her.

Paul moved impatiently, and she was reminded that he had asked a question.

'Yes, I was in fact half inclined to walk on the beach,' she answered belatedly.

'Because you could not sleep you came out here.' The same dry challenge was there although he did not add to his words. He thought it was because of him that she could not sleep. Was he inwardly jeering at her, branding her one of those who ran after him? Yet, how could he when she was so determined to go home at the end of the week? She could have stayed, at his invitation.

'I admit I could not have slept,' she returned, vitally aware of him as a man, of the fact that they were alone here, in this isolated, romantic place, sheltered, and yet with a view to the argent-sprayed seashore and the sleepy lagoon.

She recalled that Mark Twain had declared that: 'God made Mauritius first and then Heaven, Heaven being copied from Mauritius.'

She heard Paul say, very softly . . . almost gently, 'Where are your thoughts, Emma?'

'I was thinking of Mark Twain and what he said about this lovely island.'

He nodded his head but said nothing, and after a while, Emma asked him how he came to be here.

'Did you ever live in France?' she added finally, and he shook his head.

'We've been here for generations. We're blanc Mauritians, not French.'

'Oh, yes, I knew that; Louise told me. But I wondered if you'd lived in France.'

'Originally we came over from France but a long time ago.'

She fell silent, mind confused, because with one part of it she wanted to escape to the safety of her room, but with the other part she wanted to stay. And yet if she did stay, whether by her own intention or his, there would be only one sequel. . . .

Safety was best, and she said, with an unconscious, little plea in her voice, 'Let me pass, Paul—' And then she stopped, remembering that she'd resolved never to address him as Paul again.

'Not yet,' he said and took her arm. 'I was intending to take a stroll on the beach so we might as well go together.'

'No, I—'

'Afraid again?'

'No, but. . . .' She glanced up to see his expression, it was unreadable but for the ironical twist to his lips. 'I really am tired,' she ended, unaware of the plea in her wide, limpid eyes. 'Do let me pass.'

His response was to tighten his hold on her arm and say, 'Walk with me, Emma. I shan't be able to sleep either.'

She had begun to shake her head, but the second sentence brought her up with a jerk. What was he trying to convey? There was incalculable quality about his words, and his expression was equally as puzzling.

She said slowly, 'I shouldn't have thought that you would ever have difficulty in sleeping.' Emma found herself being gently propelled forward, and offering no resistance.

'Why?' he queried briefly.

'Because you haven't anything on your mind.'

He shot her a glance from his superior height.

'And how, might I ask, do you know that?'

She coloured up.

'I suppose I took it for granted that you hadn't worrying things on your mind,' she said. They were walking slowly towards the gate leading onto the deserted shore, her mind in turmoil because she could not understand this altogether new attitude he was showing towards her. It was only a short while ago that he had been giving all his attention to the lovely Eileen.

'What things have you on your mind that are so worrying?' inquired Paul after a long silence and the absence of any comment on what Emma had said.

'I suppose . . . nothing much, really,' she replied a little lamely, because she knew she was lying to him. But she could scarcely be honest and admit that it was *he* who was on her mind and that she was confused by feelings she wouldn't have analysed even if she could. 'Not now that Louise has agreed to come home with me.'

'So your sister's welfare was worrying you?'

'You know it was, for otherwise I'd not have been begging you to sack her.'

'I think you have other problems, Emma,' he said blandly after a while. And, when she did not answer he added with a hint of persuasion, 'Stay here; you know you'd like to—'

'We've gone into that,' she broke in swiftly. 'It's impossible.'

'No such thing. In fact it's more than ever possible now that your sister has decided to go home. Any slight risk there was of her finding out will be dispelled.'

'If you continue to talk like this,' she said tersely, 'I shan't walk with you.'

'But you will if I don't?' He was amused, and it showed in his tone.

'I wish I could understand your mood,' she almost snapped, not having meant to say anything like that but her nerves were all awry, for this situation was too intimate, the surroundings too romantic . . . and Paul's magnetism too powerful by far.

'My mood?' Paul slanted an eyebrow and added

smoothly, 'I am sure you know that I'm in a mood to kiss you—' And the next moment she was in his arms, her mouth possessed by moist demanding lips that crushed hers in a long and passionate kiss that left her fighting for breath. She tried to struggle but gave up, lacking even a modicum of strength that would compare with his. He held her very close; her soft breasts flattened against the muscled hardness of his chest, and both his hands were sliding downwards, caressing her thighs, lingering for a few seconds before continuing their masterful and possessive progress until sensuous, seeking fingers reached their target. Emma shuddered in ecstasy against him, arching her slender body to meld it with his. She was conscious of the heady, male smell of him mingling with that now familiar brand of body lotion, could feel his heart racing and, lower, his manhood rising with desire.

'Come live with me,' he quoted in a throaty bass tone. 'Emma, you need me as much as I need you so don't throw away the pleasure you will have—'

'No!' She did not want to struggle for freedom but she did, his words flashing sanity into her mind if not her body. But her mind could control her body, she told herself fiercely, and despite the agony of longing, she began to fight him in earnest. He held her with ease for a while and then, whether in impatience or for some other reason, he let her go. She was trembling all over, her legs like rubber, and if he hadn't caught her to him again she would most certainly have fallen, or at best, staggered drunkenly to find support by the nearest tree. Her heart was racing, her emotions so heightened that they affected every nerve cell in her body. She spoke to him in quivering accents, 'Why do you do it? I don't seem able to convince you that I don't want an affair.'

'Not an affair as such,' he agreed, much to her surprise, but went on to add, 'You want me, though, Emma, so denials would be untruths.'

'You're so sure of yourself!'

'No, dear, of you.'

Dear . . . a slip of the tongue; it meant nothing.

'Let me go back,' she begged huskily.

'Not yet—'

'Oh, but—please?'

'Don't panic,' he said with a hint of asperity. 'I'll not force myself on you. But you need to sit down for a few minutes. There's a seat on the shore just outside the gate—you've probably seen it. We'll sit there for a while.' He was already urging her forward, and soon they were sitting down, the lagoon dark and sleepy before them, the reef sparkling in the moonlight, the sails of the graceful yacht still bending in the breeze.

Emma closed her eyes tightly to hold back the cloud of tears gathering behind them.

The truth had come to her—at which precise moment she did not know, but perhaps it had been there already, hidden in her subconscious.

The truth . . . which could not be denied or cast out to be forgotten so that recovery would be swift.

'What are you thinking, Emma?' Paul's voice was low and it sounded strangely alien, attractively so. 'You are miles away from me.'

She looked at him and merely shook her head, unable to speak for the misery that seemed to rise into her chest and throat so that she was aware of a choking sensation which prevented speech.

Miles away, he had said. But she was close, sitting here . . . beside the man she had foolishly fallen in love with, a man who wanted her only as his mistress, his bedmate, a man who had already several times tried to seduce her.

'If you are feeling better now,' she heard him say, 'we'll go back.'

'Yes, I'm ready.' Her tone was dull and he turned swiftly to look at her.

'Are you all right?' He sounded anxious, she thought and immediately answered him.

'I'm okay, now, thank you.'

'You're pale,' he observed and fingered her cheek lightly.

'I'm tired.' She knew her manner was cool and short, but she wanted to get away from him, to the bedroom where she could release the painful pressure behind her eyes.

He took her arm but moved away as they neared the house. Emma looked upwards instinctively. Eileen was standing on the verandah of her bedroom, looking down at them. She waved, then called, 'Paul, I'd like to go in for a swim. Are you coming, too?'

A second's hesitation before Paul answered, a smile on his lips, 'Yes, I'll join you. Give me ten minutes or so.'

Emma's lips quivered; she just had to say, 'You're still not tired apparently.'

'Very wide awake, in fact.' He looked down into her eyes and added with what could only be described as a grim inflection, 'Contrary to what you believe, I do have troublesome things on my mind.'

She glanced away.

Not nearly so troublesome as mine, she thought, and bade him a brief good night.

'I hope you can sleep this time,' he said on opening the front door for her to precede him into the hall. 'You look as if you could do with a good night's rest.'

Something beyond her control made her say tartly,

'Your concern's very touching, Paul, but quite unnecessary.' And on that parting shot she left him, hurrying up the stairs.

Chapter Seven

Eileen was sunning herself on the lawn, a book on the grass beside her brightly-flowered lounger. Louise and Emma had lunched out at an hotel, and now Louise had gone off to collect Jeremy, Emma declining to accompany her because she wanted to wash a few smalls and handkerchiefs in readiness for packing.

'I might as well do them here as take them home soiled,' she had said, and so Louise had gone off on her own.

The washing done and drying on a line at the back of the chateau, Emma was now on her verandah, watching the lovely girl with a brooding expression.

That Eileen was keen on Paul was plain, but his feelings for her were by no means so plain. With only two days left of her stay at the chateau, Emma was becoming more and more depressed, tormented by the knowledge that once she had left she would never see Paul again. There were times when she felt she could abandon everything and accept his offer, and she could only hope, as the time passed, that common sense would prevail and she would remain immune to the temptation to become Paul's mistress.

He had not tried to tempt her since that night—was it only four nights ago!—when she had been so deeply affected by his lovemaking that he had sat her down to relax. In fact, he had treated her with near indifference, and she could now fully understand just how her sister had once felt—the sheer hopelessness, the misery and the frustration that resulted from the knowledge that one was powerless to penetrate the hard core of Paul's personality.

Paul came into her vision now, distinguished even in casual slacks and the pearl-grey shirt to match— open-necked and short-sleeved.

He swung along towards where Eileen was sitting, and Emma drew back into her bedroom.

Madame Fanchette had gone off to visit an old friend, so Emma and Louise had already said goodbye to her. But Pierre was still here, very friendly with Louise, and Emma began to wonder if anything would come of it. It was a bridge to be crossed later, though. For the time being Louise would be at home with her mother, and for that, Emma was more than a little thankful.

'I think we shall dine out this evening,' suggested

SPELL OF THE ISLAND 111

Louise much later, after the little boy had been put to bed, Emma as usual having read a story to him. As the time went by she was more and more concerned about him, for he did seem to have an affection for Louise despite her shortcomings as a nanny since coming to live in Paul's home.

Emma had asked Paul if he had done anything about a replacement and had received an abrupt, 'In my own good time, Emma. There's no need for you to concern yourself about it.'

'Dine out?' She asked Louise what restaurant she had in mind.

'The Tropicana in Curepipe. I feel sure Paul will let us have the car. In fact, I needn't ask, as he's already said I can use it.'

'All right. It'll be a nice change to have dinner out.'

However, it transpired that Paul was again to invite the sisters to dine with him and his two guests. Remembering how she was the odd one out last time—after Madame Fanchette had left, that was—Emma would have declined; but Louise seemed eager to accept, and Emma surmised the reason to be Pierre. . . .

'You didn't seem too keen on accepting my invitation.' Paul and Emma had met on the landing when she and he emerged from their bedrooms together, his room being two doors away from hers.

'We'd talked of going out,' she returned. 'It would have been a change, seeing that we're leaving the day after tomorrow.'

His brow darkened at that reminder, and she strongly suspected that despite his interest in Eileen, he still desired Emma for his mistress.

'Perhaps we could all dine out,' he mused after a small silence and, staggered by the suggestion, Emma shot him a questioning glance.

'All of us?' she frowned. 'But why should you bother changing your plans just for Louise and me?'

The dark eyes became veiled.

'I'm not changing them. As a matter of fact, I had thought of taking you out to dine before you left.'

'Me . . . or my sister as well.' She was all suspicion without quite knowing what she had to be suspicious about.

He quirked her a smile. This was more like his old self, she thought, coolly sardonic with a degree of amused mockery. It suddenly occurred to Emma that she felt more comfortable than when he became deep and serious.

'Always suspecting me of some ulterior motive, aren't you, Emma. If I did take you out alone what possible danger could you be in?'

She hesitated about entering into his mood, dejected as she was. But the temptation was too much for her and she retorted with, 'I'd be alone with you in the car—and there are many dark and lonely lanes between here and a town.'

He laughed, and she caught her breath as always. Really, it was no wonder women found him irresistible, she mused, waiting for him to speak.

'Your opinion of me isn't very high, is it?' he said.

'Should it be? After the way you have treated me?'

'You reciprocated—'

'Can we change the subject?' Emma sent him a glowering look. 'If you want Louise and me to have dinner here with you and your guests, then we accept—we already have accepted, so I don't see what all the argument is about.'

'That temper,' murmured Paul with mock severity. 'I ought to help you curb it.'

'We were talking about dinner tonight,' she reminded him acidly. 'Please keep to the subject.'

He asked curiously, 'What made you accept if you'd already decided to dine out?'

'It was Louise—she wanted to—to. . . .' Emma stopped herself but obviously not in time for her companion said sardonically, 'So it is Pierre on whom your sister has now set her sights, eh? How fickle women are.'

'I don't suppose for one moment Louise is expecting anything to come from the slight friendship which has sprung up between them.'

'I shall have to give my brother a talking to,' he murmured as if to himself, and Emma felt her temper rise.

'My sister's not a gold digger, no matter what you think!' she flashed. 'I shall be glad when we're away from here—and I wish I didn't have to dine with you tonight—in fact,' she went on as the idea shot into her mind, 'I shall decline your invitation and eat on my own! Louise can dine with you if she wants, either here or at an hotel, but count me out!' and on that furious note she swung on her heels and walked swiftly away, back into her bedroom.

She was trembling with anger, but crying too; she could not stem the tears that came swiftly to her eyes.

She cursed the fate that had decreed she and Paul

should bump into one another like that. Now she had the difficult task of telling her sister that she had opted out of the dinner invitation. Louise was bound to ask questions—Her thoughts were cut, and her eyes flew to the door as she heard a knock on the panel. Paul surely wouldn't. . . .

'Can I come in, Emma?' Louise was in the doorway, her hair in rollers. 'Did you bring a dryer with you?' she asked hopefully. 'Something's gone wrong with mine. . . . Is anything the matter? You look—furious.'

'No, I'm all right.' She paused a moment, forgetting the dryer. 'About this evening, Louise—I've decided not to come to dinner. I'd rather have something here, in my room—a sandwich will do.'

Louise closed the door and came into the room.

'There must be some reason. We've accepted Paul's invitation, so he'll be expecting us to dine with him and the other two.'

'He'll be expecting you, but not me.' She looked down at the carpet, avoiding her sister's puzzled gaze. 'I've told him I shan't be there.'

There was an odd expression in Louise's eyes, as well there might be, for this was certainly unexpected. She said slowly, 'Have you and Paul had words, or something?'

'We have.' There seemed nothing for it but to say outright that she had lost her temper with Paul and told him she was dining on her own. But of course this led naturally to the further question: what had they quarrelled about? 'I can't tell you, Louise, so don't waste your breath on pursuing the matter. I wish we were leaving here tonight!'

'Why were you crying?'

Emma's teeth snapped together.

'I've told you not to question me,' she said, marvelling that she could keep her voice steady for she was all churned up inside. 'Please leave me,' she begged. 'I'm not in the mood for company—oh, the dryer: yes, I'll get it from the bathroom.'

A moment later she was handing it to Louise, conscious of her puzzlement, her surprise that Emma should have spoken to her like that.

'I don't feel like dining without you.' Louise toyed with the dryer. 'Let's go out, as we said we would,' she suddenly added decisively. 'I think a change is what you need.'

'But—Pierre?'

Louise's eyes widened.

'Pierre?' she echoed blankly. 'What about him?'

'I thought—' Emma looked nonplussed. 'I took it for granted that you'd enjoy his company. . . .' She tailed off lamely.

'You thought I was—keen on him?'

'Forget it, Louise. I came to a wrong conclusion, that's all. Do you really want to go out, then?'

'Of course. But about Pierre—we do enjoy each other's company, but, Emma, I don't happen to have a crush on him. I assure you I'm off the Fanchettes as far as anything like *that* is concerned.' She looked at Emma with sudden perception. 'You didn't quarrel with Paul about me, did you?'

Emma gave a start.

'What makes you ask that?' she prevaricated.

Louise smiled thinly.

'You seem surprised at my intelligence—oh, I can

understand, seeing that I never have been as bright as you, Emma—'

'Louise—'

'I'm not offended,' she laughed. 'It's out of character for me to cotton on like that. But I know, somehow, that I was the cause of your quarrel with Paul, and that his brother had something to do with it. And having deduced that much, it isn't difficult to guess that Paul made one of his caustic remarks to the effect that I was running after Pierre.' She looked at her sister for confirmation and yet denied her the chance of commenting as she continued, 'Thank you for defending me, Emma. It was good of you, especially as you yourself believed I was keen on Pierre.'

'You must admit,' Emma just had to say, 'that you and Pierre do get along very well together.'

'I like him very much, but I'm keeping my heart in its right place—at least for the time being.'

Emma had to laugh at her phrasing, and as Louise joined in, the whole situation was eased. They decided to go out to dinner; but Louise had been glancing through a brochure, and she had noticed that there was dancing nightly at the Saint Geran, an hotel reputed to be the most exclusive—and expensive—on the island.

'Let's go there,' she urged. 'My treat.'

'No, mine.'

'We'll go dutch,' decided Louise and hastened away with the hair dryer.

The hotel was all it was made out to be—and more. Situated on what Emma felt was the most beautiful beach she would ever see, it was a low, sprawling building surrounded by exotic gardens where fountains played, where multicoloured fish swam in ornamental pools where water lilies abounded. Rockeries and cascades, tropical flowers and bushes, flame trees and Royal palms, junipers with their beautiful rose-coloured highly perfumed timber, variegated bamboos striped with vivid green, the orchid trees and Indian walnut trees—the variety was endless. Flowers, too, grew in abundance around immaculately tended lawns or in beds and borders or round the ornamental pools.

Both Emma and Louise were tempted to take a stroll along the beach, as they had arrived with plenty of time in hand, not having booked to dine until nine o'clock. The translucent water was shimmering in the starlight, the sand beneath their feet smooth as silk. Palms along the backshore and tamarinds, graceful and delicate, foliage fluttering in the breeze, the cooling trade-wind breeze so welcome after the heat of the day.

'It's fantastic!' breathed Emma. 'Like paradise!'

'I'd love to live on the island,' sighed Louise, 'but that won't ever be possible.'

'No. . . .' Paul's face rising up before her, that twisted smile which spelt cynicism . . . and perhaps disillusionment, she mused as she recalled that he had once been let down by his fiancée.

'I wish we had a bit longer.' Louise was taking off her sandals to walk barefoot in the gentle sand. 'Let's come next year, and stay here, at the Saint Geran.'

'It would be too expensive.'

'Oh, I don't know. We could come off-season, I expect.'

'I'd like to bring Mother; she needs a break.' Emma was holding her dress up, because she kept treading on the hem.

'We'll have to think about it,' decided Louise who, thought Emma, seemed to have become more mature within a matter of days.

They made their way back, and Louise put her sandals on again. The path through the illuminated gardens was bordered by brilliant, magenta bougainvillaea and hibiscus bushes with in between smaller bushes of allamandas, golden against the vivid crimson crotons.

'Let's have a drink at the pool bar,' suggested Emma after glancing at her watch. 'We've still half an hour to kill.'

The bar was busy, lit by coloured lights hidden in the trees surrounding it. But, nevertheless, there were seats for everyone if they wanted them; but the two girls stood at the bar and soon were chatting to two young men who had arrived that day from the Seychelles where they had spent one week of their two-week holiday. It was a spontaneous situation, all being in the holiday mood, and it seemed not in the least out of the ordinary when the girls agreed to have dinner with the two men after one of them, Jake, had suggested it.

And so the two small tables were put together by an obliging waiter who later came to take their orders.

'It's nice having company.' Bill, the younger man, dark and rugged with clear, healthy skin and a broad smile, passed the remark as he sat opposite to Louise at the table which was conveniently close to the dance space. 'Pity you're both going home on Saturday.'

'Here come the menus,' from Jake, who had fair, faintly gingery hair and eyebrows, blue eyes and a wide, generous mouth. 'I think I shall try the local food.'

'The Creole dishes are hot,' warned Louise, 'so be careful what you choose.'

'I happen to like hot, spicy food. . . .' He concentrated on the menu and presently ordered meat cooked with turmeric, aniseed, hot pimentos and mango, all served with the customary saffron rice. His friend chose something more conventional— grilled steak with patisson and baby marrows.

'I'm having *coeur de palmiste*,' decided Louise. 'Of all the time I've been here I haven't yet tried the famous palm hearts.'

'They're not plentiful,' put in the waiter who had been standing by. 'You see, the hearts have to come from a seven-year-old palm. So you see, it is a rare savoury and not always on the menu. You are in luck!'

Emma had *camarons*—freshwater prawns caught locally—and a selection of green vegetables.

The men chose the wine, a fruity white imported from France.

Between courses the four got up to dance, and it was during one of these most pleasant interludes that Emma gave a little gasp which made her partner hold her away and look at her askance.

'My sister's employer,' she elucidated, 'with his

brother and—and a friend.' Eileen looked glorious! All heads turned to stare at the regal figure clad in slinky silver lamé with diamonds sparkling in her hair and at her throat. She wore several bracelets, too, one of exquisite sapphires and diamonds.

'Phew!' exclaimed Jake. 'Are those sparklers real?' He had followed the direction of Emma's gaze and was now scarcely moving as he fixed his attention on the girl who was attracting so much notice, especially from the men. She had a hand on Paul's sleeve, possessively, it seemed to Emma who decided that her evening was now at least partly spoiled. Paul had elected to bring his guests out to dinner, and it was a quirk of fate that he had chosen the same hotel as the girls. And yet, thinking about it, Emma had to own that the most exclusive and expensive hotel would be his obvious choice.

He was just sitting down at the table to which he and his companions had been conducted when he spotted Emma, and she saw his eyes widen and then narrow to mere slits. She shuddered involuntarily and then was angry that she should be affected by what was plainly his displeasure.

Did he think he owned the place!

'Have you seen what the wind's blown in?' said Louise with a grimace when Emma and her partner were sitting down at the table. 'Eileen's making an exhibition of herself if you ask me. I should hate being the focus of attention like that! And I don't admire Paul for escorting her in that sexy getup.'

Everyone laughed including Emma, but as her eyes caught those of the other girl her laughter died. Eileen might have been looking at a servant—and wondering how on earth she had managed to get in here! Emma's chin tilted, her eyes sparkled. Paul noticed the interplay and seemed both interested and amused. But there was that about him—the flexed jaw and compressed mouth—which plainly illustrated his inner anger.

'He looks like thunder,' commented Louise a moment later as his veneer of amusement faded. 'I wonder what's up with him. Maybe he's not too happy with his girl friend's sexy outfit after all.'

Emma said nothing; she had suddenly resolved to ignore that particular table and enjoy herself.

However, she had not reckoned with Paul's coming over to ask her to dance. Completely taken aback, she opened her mouth to refuse, then thought better of it, because it would be in the nature of a snub and she was disinclined to do a thing like that.

She rose unsteadily, glad that Louise was dancing already with Jake. Emma was swung into Paul's arms, and any fears she had concerning her own inadequacy were swiftly dispelled as she and he glided round the floor in perfect harmony, almost as if they were one.

For a long moment Paul remained quiet, with Emma aware of a tension which profoundly affected her nerves.

At last he spoke and his voice was harsh-edged and imperious.

'Why didn't you say you and Louise had a date?'

'We hadn't—'

'Hadn't?' he snapped before she could continue. 'Then who are these two?'

She looked up into a face taut and rather frightening. This was yet another of his many moods that went to make up the complexity of his nature. Emma was beginning to think that blanc Maritians were very strange people.

'We've only just met them—well, a short while ago—at the bar,' she explained innocently. 'So we decided to have dinner togeth—'

'You mean—you picked them up!' he rasped, and she had a strong suspicion that he would dearly love to shake her . . . or something worse. 'You actually picked up two men—in a bar?'

Count ten, Emma. . . . She wished her temper would not flare like this! But it was only with this man; no other human being had aroused in her the resentment and anger which Paul did and it suddenly occurred to her that even if—by some miracle—he fell in love with her and married her, they would without doubt lead a cat and dog life!

She said at last, marvelling at her control, 'It really has nothing to do with you, Paul, now has it?'

If this mild manner surprised him he gave no evidence of it as he said, 'You're a guest in my home and, therefore, I have a right to expect you to behave with at least a small amount of decorum and propriety.'

She wanted to laugh at the stiffness which was so reminiscent of his manner with her right at the beginning, when first she was introduced to him, and she wondered if he ever unbent.

However, it behoved her to keep a straight face, and this she managed to do. Her tones were still mild when presently she answered him.

'It was not picking up, Paul. We were all in a holiday spirit and after all, lots of people get talking in bars. We chatted and the result was that the young men suggested we all dine together.'

He was silent for a space, but she had the impression that he was gritting his teeth.

'I invited you both out to dinner, if you remember?' His voice was harsh and low; he suddenly drew her close, not at all gently, as another couple glided too near to them.

'Then we had a disagreement, if you remember?' she ended, stealing his question.

'About nothing, as things have turned out.'

'So you take back your accusation against my sister?'

'I cannot recollect accusing her of anything.'

'You *implied*, then, that she was running after Pierre.'

'I admit I was wrong.'

'Good heavens!' she could not help exclaiming. 'You are actually admitting a thing like that! There's hope for you, yet!' She stopped rather abruptly, staggered by her temerity. Paul looked down into her flushed face and said in a dangerously soft voice, 'Careful, Emma. If I had you home at this moment, I'd shake you till your teeth chattered.'

'No need to tell me that,' she returned. 'Your expression's enough.'

She heard his furious intake of breath, winced as his fingers at her back pressed ruthlessly into her flesh. What a strange situation this was! Intimate, just as so many other moments had been intimate, with each saying exactly what they wanted, without any attempt at diplomacy or a sparing of the other's feelings.

The music stopped, and he escorted her back to her table and left her without a glance at the other three sitting there.

It was only natural that Louise should at the first opportunity ask what was going on.

'Paul's whole manner with you when you were dancing was odd,' she continued when, the meal finished, they went to the powder room. 'He seemed —sort of—proprietorial, as if he were telling you off with a vengeance.'

'He was annoyed that we had joined Jake and Bill.'

'Annoyed!' Louise blinked at her, lip rouge poised in midair. 'What the devil has it to do with him?'

Emma shrugged her shoulders.

'He seemed to think it has, seeing I'm a guest in his home. He said he expected me to act with decorum.'

Louise stared at her strangely through the mirror.

'There's something I don't understand, isn't there, Emma?' she said quietly.

'That makes two of us,' was Emma's flat response. 'Paul's an enigma.'

'He seemed rather familiar.' Louise's expression was unfathomable as she added slowly and deliberately, 'He was calling you Emma almost from the beginning which surprised me exceedingly.'

Emma took a comb from her evening bag and drew it through her hair.

'I'd rather not talk about Paul,' she returned. 'After Saturday we shall never see him again.'

'Just what are you hiding?' Louise used the lip rouge and put it away. 'There's something between you—'

'No such thing!' broke in Emma, hoping she was convincing, but she very much doubted it. 'I don't know how you've managed to get that idea.'

'You're not very clever at deceit, but then you've never had to practise it before—at least, not to my knowledge. Even now you're blushing—'

'Louise, please let the matter drop!'

'You've fallen for him.' A statement without a trace of bitterness or anger. 'So now you see how dangerously attractive he is.' She paused, but Emma, very pale now as, the colour having receded from her cheeks as swiftly as it had appeared, had nothing to say and her sister went on, 'Paul isn't totally immune, though. I'm sure he finds something attractive in you. Be careful, Emma, or he'll have you doing something you'll regret.'

Emma looked at her, thinking again how mature she had become. She said quietly, 'As we shall be leaving the chateau on Saturday there won't be much time for me to do anything I'll regret, will there?'

Louise allowed that to pass without comment.

'You haven't denied anything I've said—oh, except you were very emphatic about there being nothing between you. But otherwise, well, you haven't made any protest so I presume I'm right in what I've said?'

'Once and for all, Louise, I am not talking about

Paul! Come on, the men will be waiting for us; we promised to have a flutter with them in the Casino.'

'Roulette? It terrifies me!'

'Nonsense; you can't possibly lose much if you put your counters on the corners. You have four chances of winning that way.'

Louise looked at her in astonishment.

'How do you know this? You've never yet seen the inside of a Casino.'

'I learned it from a card I picked up in the lobby here. It's in my bag if you want to read it. It tells you—wait, I'll show it to you.' She took it from her bag and handed it to Louise. 'You can't go wrong because they've given you a diagram, and below are the stakes and odds.'

Louise took a cursory look and handed the card back.

'That's all very well until you get inside, and then what? We're going to look darned silly playing with a few chips placed on the corners while the experienced gamblers use stacks.'

'I daresay they are used to novices like us,' returned Emma who was in fact looking forward to the flutter. She might have beginner's luck, but even if she didn't, it would be an experience she might never have again.

It was to transpire that she won almost every time, and when at last they all came away from the table, she had won rupees to the equivalent of twenty-two pounds.

'Aren't you lucky,' commented Jake. 'I've lost about five pounds.'

'I've lost too,' from Bill. 'Oh, well, never mind.

Lucky at gambling unlucky in love—' He stopped and laughed. 'Only a quotation, Emma, and I believe I have it wrong anyway.'

Unlucky in love. . . .

Emma felt the prick of tears and prayed that Saturday would come quickly.

Chapter Eight

The following morning Emma went for a swim before breakfast; the sun was already painting the tropical landscape with gold, and bright birds darted about, stealing colour, changing it.

So peaceful! Yet Emma's mind was in turmoil. She had lain awake, and when eventually in the early hours her restlessness had ceased, it was only because she had half made up her mind to stay in Mauritius, accepting Paul's offer.

But with the light of day a very different aspect presented itself, and she saw vividly the time when Paul tired of her, when the first signs would be indifference, perhaps a sharp word, or even worse, long silences. And then that dreaded moment when he would say it was all ended.

And she would leave, her life shattered, for no other man could ever replace him.

She entered the water, so warm and smooth around her honey-tanned flesh; she tried to forget everything and live for the moment. But fate decreed otherwise. She saw Paul swinging along, towel dangling, wrap open and belt trailing on the sand. Tall, erect, striding along with that especial athletic grace which stamped him as nobility. His head was held high, shoulders broad and square. Emma swam to the shore, hoping to get her wrap, pick up her towel, and with no more than a brief and polite 'good morning' make her escape.

Paul reached the place where she had left her things before she did, and she bit her lip. His face was set and stern, eyes hard and steely dark. She guessed he was thinking of last night.

'Good morning,' she said into the silence. 'You're—going in for a swim. You're early . . . I'm j-just coming out. . . .' The disjointed sentences brought a slight relaxing of his features as the ghost of a smile touched his mouth.

'Running away, as usual.' Paul's voice was sardonic, his eyes inscrutable as they wavered from her flushed face to the delicate outline of her breasts and then back again.

'I'm not escaping, as you term it,' denied Emma, trying to recover her composure. 'I've had my swim, so naturally I want to go in and have my shower.'

'Had your swim?' The straight black brows were raised. 'You haven't been in the water for more than three minutes at most.'

'How do you know that?'

'Because I was at my bedroom window when you came from the chateau. It didn't take more than three minutes for me to get into my trunks and coat, so—'

'You followed me deliberately?'

'It's nice to have company on one's early morning swim,' was his suave response. 'Come on—'

'No! I'm going in!'

'You're the most hot-tempered woman I have ever known.' His voice was mild and unfathomable.

Emma said, looking down to where he stood in front of her wrap, 'If you'll step aside, I can get my things.'

At that he gave a low laugh which erased any sternness that had remained.

'Afraid to get them? Afraid of coming too close?'

Emma clenched her fists.

'Just what do you get out of this game you play with me?' she demanded.

'Strangely, not very much,' was his astonishing admission and he seemed to heave a sigh.

The moment was tense, electric, with Emma having the strange conviction that if only she could adopt the right attitude, say the right thing, her whole future would be affected. What was this elusive thing within her? Perhaps her subconscious was urging her to accept Paul's offer . . . perhaps if she did so, Paul, instead of tiring of her, would come to realise he could not do without her. The idea persisted, but yet, she could not produce the words she believed Paul wanted to hear.

She spoke into the silence, asking again if he

would move, and adding before he could speak, 'If you want company on your swim, then why didn't you ask your girl friend to come with you?' Emma could not have explained those words, for she hated the idea that Eileen was in fact Paul's girl friend. She saw the dark eyes flicker curiously, the slight tilt of the head as if in silent inquiry, the unfathomable set of the mouth.

'And what,' came the smooth voice at last, 'has given you the idea that Eileen is my girl friend?'

As there was no drawing back now, Emma found herself saying, aware now that she had referred to Eileen as his girl friend in order to note his reaction.

'I took it for granted. Your mother seems to like her,' she added, feeling somewhat specious, since she would not have said this had she not overheard that conversation between mother and son.

'My mother likes her?' with that lift of an eyebrow again. 'I wasn't aware that you'd had an opportunity to observe my mother's attitude towards Eileen,' he said with an enigmatic inflection. 'Apart from your dining with us on one occasion, where else can your observations have been made?'

She averted her eyes, aware of colour tinting her cheeks. How easily this man could always set her at a disadvantage!

'Forget it,' she almost snapped, more angry with herself than him, for it was she who had capriciously mentioned Eileen.

'Evasion, eh?' There was a hint of mockery in the rich voice now. He bent to pick up her wrap. 'I wonder what made you mention Eileen in the first place?' he murmured inscrutably. And, without

affording her a chance to reply—even had she a
reply ready, which of course she hadn't—he added
almost imperiously, 'Turn around and I'll help you
into this covering. Your embarrassment is obvious to
me, though I doubt if you yourself are aware of it.'
Again that mockery, tinged with amusement this
time as his eyes flickered to where her hands lay
clasped below her stomach, in an unconscious position of modesty. Naturally his remark made her
blush, and she would have snatched the beach coat
from him, but he deftly caught her wrist, jerking her
to him. The kiss was brief and hard.

'Pity we can be seen from the house,' he said as
with warm hands on her damp shoulders, he turned
her round.

'I wish I could understand you,' said Emma in a
sort of petulant, complaining voice when having put
the wrap on her, he began tying the belt, his dark
eyes boring into her, an impassiveness about them
which was as puzzling as the almost tender curve of
his mouth.

Did he care—? No . . . was he *beginning* to care?
If she became his mistress would he learn to love
her? Was the risk too great or should she take a
gamble where the result would be all or nothing?

Paul had finished tying the belt and drew away.
Emma sensed that he had been considering her
words but that he had now dismissed them from his
mind. His next words confirmed this.

'Are you sure you want to go? Three minutes in
the water's not much.'

'Yes, I want to go—' She stopped, half wishing she
hadn't lied because in any case Paul, with his keen

perception, would be well aware that, deep down, she really did want to swim with him. Again his words were a confirmation of her thoughts.

'You're a great little fighter, Emma, but it's not very pleasant to go against your inclinations.'

'You're so smart, aren't you!' she flashed, that temper flaring again. 'And swelled-headed.'

'Not swelled-headed,' he denied. 'Just perceptive of your transparency.' His voice was bland and faintly mocking. Emma set her teeth and flashed back at him,

'I wish *you* were as transparent, but you're an enigma! You seem to enjoy being mysterious! Well, I shan't have to put up with it for much longer, thank heaven!' and with that impolite remark she picked up her towel and walked swiftly away from him.

While having breakfast with Louise and Jeremy, Emma suggested that she and Louise go into Port Louis after Jeremy was dropped at school, as Emma wanted to buy a couple more presents for friends with whom she worked.

'I can't,' returned Louise, obviously disappointed. 'It's a short day for Jeremy. The little ones finish at noon, because the older ones are having their sports' practice this afternoon.'

'Oh.' Emma became thoughtful. 'You could drop me in Port Louis, though, if you don't mind going all that way, and I could get a taxi back.'

Louise was hesitating, and just as Emma was about to say it didn't matter, she would drop the idea, her sister spoke.

'I feel I should spend this morning getting all

Jeremy's clothes in order, and the nursery looking spick-and-span, ready for the next nanny. I'd hate to think that Paul could find anything to complain about.'

Emma nodded in agreement.

'I'll not bother, then,' she decided. 'I'll help you with the nursery.'

'You could go both ways by taxi,' suggested Louise but then added that it would be expensive.

'Too expensive,' agreed Emma and gave up the idea of going into town.

But it was to transpire that, by some strange coincidence, and just as if he had known of Emma's desire, Paul came to her as she sat on a lounger in the sunshine, reading a book. Louise had asked if she wanted to go with her to school, for the ride, but Emma had declined. She would relax in the garden, she decided. She glanced up as Paul approached, surprised at his smile in view of the way she had spoken to him earlier. It seemed he had not taken offence by it.

'I don't suppose you'd like to go into town?' he asked, eyes flickering and interested as they took in the revealing sun top and brief shorts. Not difficult to see where his sensuous thoughts were! 'Eileen and I are going into Port Louis. She has some shopping to do, and I have some business I want to attend to.'

Yes, he had an office in Port Louis, recalled Emma, and he had an apartment there as well. . . .

'I did intend going into town,' she admitted, not too keen on going along with Eileen but at the same time knowing she would feel better if she did get the presents she wanted. 'But Louise couldn't come, as Jeremy finishes school at noon today.' She had laid her book aside on the grass and was sitting upright. He could feast his eyes on *less* that way!

'Then you must come along with us. I shall be coming back at about three this afternoon.'

Emma slanted him an upward glance.

'You?' she said. 'Won't Eileen be coming back with you?'

Paul quirked her a perceptive smile and shook his head.

'No, she's staying in Port Louis tonight with a friend. So you'll have me all to yourself on the way back,' he added in some amusement after a slight pause.

He expected an acid retort from Emma and was not disappointed. But in her anger Emma spoke words that left her wide open to a riposte that sent the blood rushing to her face.

'That'll be an exciting experience for me!'

'I can make it so, Emma . . . so exciting you'll remember it for a long time. As you once said, there are lots of lonely places between here and town.'

'I don't want your lift after all,' she snapped, putting cool palms to her hot cheeks. 'I've changed my mind!'

'Don't be silly.' A dramatic change in him all at once and she rather thought that he regretted goading her to the point where she would refuse his offer of a lift. 'You know very well I'll not molest you—'

'Do I? A statement like that amazes me! Your memory must be very short.'

'Let us not start another slanging match, Emma. If I give you my promise, will that put your mind at rest?'

The temptation to remain stubborn was very

great, simply because she knew for sure that he would continue in his efforts to persuade her, and she would like to see just how far he would go. However, she decided against it and said more quietly, 'All right, I'll come with you.'

'Good. I shall be leaving in about half an hour.' He smiled down at her, and her heart caught. What an incomprehensible man he was! Suddenly she was recalling something she had read which was on a temple at Delphi in Greece: 'Know Thyself.'

Emma was of the opinion, as she watched him striding away over the lawn, that Paul Fanchette did not know himself!

'So how,' she murmured quite audibly, 'can *I* expect to know or understand him?'

Eileen was already in the front passenger seat when Emma arrived at the place where Paul usually left his car, and as he came up at that same moment he opened a rear door for her. Emma smiled as she glanced up, and he responded. But during the drive his conversation was mainly with the lovely girl sitting beside him. On reaching Port Louis he wasted no time in leaving the girls as, glancing at his watch, he realised he was already a little late for his appointment. Eileen suggested they go into a nearby cafe and have morning coffee, and Emma reluctantly agreed, much preferring to go off immediately on her own. She was to be back at the car at three, and she wanted to have a wander around the town before making her purchases.

The cafe was outdoors, beneath the trees in the square. Eileen was soon asking Emma questions about herself, her interest seeming to be out of all proportion. Emma passed most of them off effectively and without being too cool with the girl. But when she was asked what she thought of Paul, she stiffened immediately and said with a chill inflection, 'I wouldn't dream of passing an opinion on my sister's employer, Miss Jennings. Such a thing would be quite out of place.' Finality in her tone but little did she know that, later, she was to say something about Paul that the girl would carry to him—later but not today.

'Perhaps I shouldn't have asked,' was all Eileen said to that, and for the next ten minutes or so the conversation was scanty and confined to the merits of the town.

Glad to get away, Emma made for the museum after having seen a sign directing people to it. She wanted to see the life-like model of the famous dodo, a bird made extinct in the seventeenth century when the island was occupied by those who obviously had destructive tendencies. And its name had since then been inseparable from that of Mauritius, its being figured in the Arms of the island and incorporated in many tourist souvenirs. She felt sad as she stood there, staring at the model, and a copy of a painting done by Savery in 1625, sad that it should be extinct. It could not fly and apart from its destruction by men, it seemingly fell prey to the newly-introduced pigs.

'Dead as a dodo. . . .' How apt the saying!

From the museum she went to the shops and strolled along, merely window-gazing at first, enjoying novel experiences and the warm sunshine. A small cafe tempted her to take a snack lunch before setting out to look for the presents she wanted. The choice was limitless, with lovely things both from Europe and the East. For one friend who made all her own clothes she bought a dress length of embroidered satin, and for the other friend a set of Indian costume jewelry—necklace, bracelet and earrings— which were packed in a velvet-lined gift box.

With still an hour to spare she wandered to the waterfront to enjoy the cool trade-wind breeze and watch the activity of the busy harbour.

Paul arrived at their meeting place only two minutes after she did; he looked at his watch and asked Emma if she would like a drive to Pamplemousses Gardens, which would take about twenty minutes. She eagerly accepted, for she had read about these world famous botanical gardens and had regretted not having asked Louise to take her there when they were in Port Louis.

Paul was oddly silent for the entire drive, but Emma was glad in a way for she was able to absorb the scenery, giving her whole attention to it.

Once at the gardens Paul parked the car, and they began a stroll which took them down long avenues, past pretty ornamental lakes, in some of which thrived the fantastic water lily of giant size, named Victoria Regia.

'It's so peaceful here,' breathed Emma feeling almost light-hearted and happy . . . with Paul beside her, friendly in a distant kind of way. Emma was grateful for small mercies; Paul and she usually had arguments, and so today was a special treat for her. A memory she would cherish for years to come. 'It's almost tangible—the atmosphere of peace and calm, I mean.'

He nodded and slanted her a glance. She wished he would hold her hand. She smiled wanly to herself, and her lip quivered.

'These gardens are famous for the rarity of many of the trees and other plants,' he told her after a while. 'They were planned by two Frenchmen, one of whom, Pierre Poivre, was so enthusiastic that he actually risked his life by smuggling spice plants from the Sundra Islands. The Dutch had already inflicted the death penalty on several people who had tried to smuggle spices from these islands.'

'You mean—the Dutch had a jealously guarded monopoly in the Sundra Islands?' She glanced up at him in disbelief. 'The death sentence—that was awful!'

'They were strange times,' he agreed, 'and stranger laws. The spices never did bring huge fortunes to Mauritius in the way they did to the Sundras,' he went on to say.

'Another plant that deserves mention,' went on Paul after another long silence, 'is the Cassava or manioc. It was brought over from Brazil as food for the slaves.'

Emma frowned, but made no comment. She was taking in the beauty of rare palms and numerous other trees and remembering that these gardens would be more beautiful still were it not for the damage done by cyclones. Even as it was, the sheer loveliness of the palm-lined avenues, the lakes, the flower-bordered little pathways, was something she knew she would never forget.

'And now we come to Paul and Virginie Avenue—' Paul turned his head to look down at her with a hint of amusement in his dark eyes. 'I expect you know all about these immortal lovers?'

'I've read about them, yes. It was a sad story.'

'A novel whose main characters have become so real that we are now approaching the legendary tomb.' Laughter in his voice and Emma thought she would never see him as attractive as he was today. But then she would not have time, seeing that she was leaving tomorrow night. 'The "tomb" is in fact a pedestal of a statue of the Goddess Flora.'

'It is easy to imagine that the story of Paul and Virginie is true, though,' mused Emma almost to herself. The couple had been brought up as neighbours on the Ile de France in the eighteenth century and grew to love one another. Virginie was sent to France to be educated, and Paul waited for her. But the *Saint Geran* on which she sailed was wrecked and Paul, standing on the shore waiting for his beloved, saw her drowned before his eyes and he died of a broken heart. 'There's been a film of Bernardin de St. Pierre's famous book,' she added, 'but I expect you already know that?'

He merely nodded his head; he seemed far away from her now, distant, aloof.

How changeable his moods!

Back in the car he again drove in silence, his profile set, his eyes staring ahead, unmoving for most of the time. Where were his thoughts? Emma wondered, thinking of the conversation she had overheard. Perhaps he was bored with his life at present and was ready for another diversion. Would he tempt Eileen to be his mistress? Or would he marry her? If his response to his mother's persuasion were anything to go by, then marriage was not at present contemplated.

Her thoughts switched, because she did not want to spoil this ride by thinking of Eileen and coupling her name with Paul's.

It was a long time later that he said, sending her a swift, sideways glance as he took his eyes off the road for a second, 'What are you thinking about, Emma?'

She had been thinking that it seemed much longer than a fortnight since she came to the Chateau Fanchette, but the answer she gave him was, 'This time tomorrow I shan't have more than a few hours left.'

Silence, profound and incomprehensible. The car seemed to be invaded by an electric current, and Emma felt her nerves tense. She looked at her companion, noticed the almost glowering expression, saw with fascinated eyes the way his hands had tightened on the wheel so that the knuckles stood out white against the teak darkness of the skin. That he was in the grip of a strong emotion seemed evident, and when he spoke it was with thinly veiled irritation.

'You appear exceedingly eager to be gone from Mauritius.' He jammed on his brakes as a car came swerving round a bend, taking up much more than half of the narrow road.

'I only came for a fortnight,' Emma reminded him, her nerves a little shaken by what had just occurred. Paul was speeding along again and she saw with an access of depression that they were nearly home.

'And I invited you to stay longer.' There was a harsh thrust to his voice, but his expression had eased, was not nearly so formidable as it had been a few moments ago.

Ignoring his remark Emma said, 'My mother's alone; she'll be glad that Louise and I are going home tomorrow.'

'You told me you didn't live at home.'

'Nevertheless, I do visit her regularly.'

Paul flashed her an obscure look.

'So you wouldn't live here under *any* circumstances?'

'Under . . . ?' Emma slid him a mystified glance. 'I don't understand. If it's a subtle way of putting your offer again, then you can forget it.'

Paul made no response, and the rest of the drive was not at all pleasant for Emma, for as on another occasion she was left with the idea that, somehow, the moment had been lost, that she had failed to say the right thing.

Deep depression dropped on her as the silence stretched, and even when Paul did break it on reaching the chateau, his voice was curiously detached and his manner distant.

'I hope you enjoyed it, Emma.'

'Yes—thank you.' He was opening the door for her; she came close as she stepped out. The nearness of him seemed only to increase her depression, and her lips quivered uncontrollably. Paul looked down into her face, and his expression became veiled. Emma managed a wan smile as she thanked him again, and she would have moved on, but he reminded her of her parcels which she had put on the back seat. 'Oh, yes. I forgot them.'

He was reaching for them; his hand brushed hers

as he gave them to her, and she quivered at the contact.

Paul closed the car door, and they went towards the chateau entrance together. Tomorrow night she would be leaving . . . so this would most likely be the last time that she and he would meet—at least, without someone else being present.

The terrible weight of dejection became almost unbearable, and tears fought for escape at the backs of her eyes. Paul glanced at her as they entered the hall, and a frown knit his brow. She felt sure he was going to ask if anything was the matter so she spoke quickly, saying she must go as she had promised to help Louise in the nursery.

Once in her room she flung herself on the bed and wept bitterly into her pillow. If only she could put the clock back for a fortnight. . . .

Chapter Nine

'So you're leaving today?" Eileen had come strolling along the beach to where Emma was sitting on a towel, having taken her last swim in the warm, tropical sea. Eileen was the last person she wanted to meet at this time when her spirits were at about their lowest ebb. However, she managed to produce a smile and said yes, she and Louise were catching the five o'clock plane.

'You've enjoyed your stay?' There was a supercilious quality about the girl's voice and an air of arrogance in her demeanour as she stood, cool and serenely lovely in an expensive, sleeveless cotton dress which unmistakably bore the stamp of Paris.

'Very much,' lied Emma, and she added for the

sake of conversation even though, from the first, she had taken a disliking to the girl, 'And you—are you enjoying your holiday?'

'Of course, but then I have Paul for company.' A small pause; Eileen's long-lashed blue eyes flickered over Emma's sun-tanned body. 'Have you a boy-friend at home?'

'No,' briefly and with that particular kind of intonation which should have put Eileen off from any further questioning, but she seemed, thought Emma, to have come here for some specific reason.

'That's a little surprising, since you are quite pretty, in a way.'

Emma frowned, more puzzled than annoyed by this patronising manner.

'Thank you,' she returned coldly.

'I have noticed your—er—attitude towards Paul. You like him, don't you?'

Emma's puzzlement grew. What on earth was the girl trying to say?

'Paul is my sister's employer—at least, his sister is. After half-past eight tonight, when we leave, she will no longer be in his employ.'

'You've avoided my question, Miss Carpenter. I am well aware that your sister has been employed here as nanny to Jeremy. You like Paul, don't you?' she persisted.

Emma pursed her lips, brow creased in thought. Something lay beneath all this, but what?

'I don't think I understand just what you are getting at,' she said, not wishing to be downright rude, but her tone was brusque for all that. She was remembering telling the girl that she would not discuss Paul.

'I've noticed how you look at him; I noticed too that there was something between you when you were dancing together. You were appearing to be having a . . . lovers' quarrel. . . .' The slow dragging of the last couple of words annoyed Emma even more than their content, although she couldn't have said why.

Her chin had lifted and there was a distinct sparkle in her eye.

'Lovers, Miss Jennings? You're insulting—but I suppose you intended to be. Perhaps you will explain why?'

The girl sat down on the warm sand, a little way from where Emma was sitting on her towel, knees now drawn up and cradled in her arms.

'Paul's philanderings are well-known to lots of people. The way you are with him has, I believe, been effective. You and he have—'

'That,' broke in Emma furiously, 'is enough! How you can dare to say such things without foundation I do not know! I do know you'll have to learn to curb that malicious tongue of yours if you want to keep out of trouble! And now, please leave me. I'd like to enjoy my last hours here.' Deliberately she turned aside, her whole body quivering with temper, and she tried to calm herself by gazing out to the tranquil sea. Colours were changing, and the water was darkening from aquamarine to emerald. It was all in the sky, she mused, reflections. . . . The sun was lowering a little; wispy clouds twisted and writhed, transparent and beautiful, golden-tinted. How she would miss it all!

A movement beside her made her jump. Lost as she was in appreciation of the beauty before her and above, she had fleetingly forgotten all about the girl sitting there.

'You still haven't answered my question,' murmured Eileen. 'Do you like Paul?'

Something snapped within Emma and she said explosively, 'I don't know why you're asking this, but the answer is no! In fact,' she added, looking at her, 'if it will please you—I detest him! And now that you have your stupid question answered will you go—' Something made her stop, for there was a sort of sneering triumph on Eileen's face. 'Just why did you ask the question?' she inquired curiously and the girl's face was instantly masked.

'That,' she answered haughtily, 'is my business.' And with that she rose gracefully and strode away.

'The girl's crazy,' declared Emma and promptly put her out of her mind.

Louise had been with Jeremy all afternoon, and it seemed to Emma that at this late stage she was regretting leaving him. The child had not been told anything, and Emma herself was troubled. Still, Jeremy was certainly adaptable, and doubtless he would soon forget both Louise and her sister.

'Well, there isn't much time left.' Emma and Louise were having their last meal; it was eight o'clock and they had to be on their way in less than an hour. Both were depressed, and the meal had been a silent one until broken by Emma with a remark that was unnecessary, but she had to say something since the silence had become oppressive.

'You can say it's ended already.' Louise heaved a deep sigh. 'I feel awfully low, Emma.' Her eyes were bright, her mouth moving convulsively.

'So do I.'

'Paul's the cause?'

'Why should you say that?'

'Because, Emma, it's very plain to see that you are in love with him—oh, not in the shallow way I was, which wasn't love at all,' she went on, obviously unaware that her words were rather muddled. 'You love him deeply, don't you?'

Emma sighed and nodded and said yes, for it was no use denying it.

'I've been a bigger fool than you,' she added and pushed her plate of stewed fruit out of the way.

'Well, I guess that this time next year you'll be able to laugh about it.'

Again Emma nodded, though she was far from sure that she would recover in a year.

'Let's get our suitcases brought down. The taxi will be here in about half an hour.' Louise drained her coffee cup and rose from the table.

'I thought you said Paul was driving us to the airport.'

'He changed his mind, said he'd have a taxi here for us instead.' So casual. Louise might be depressed, but quite plainly Paul was not the cause of *her* depression.

Emma felt she had to go in and see Jeremy, so she left her sister to get someone up to see to the suitcases.

'Don't waken him,' frowned Louise. 'Perhaps you'd better not—'

'I won't waken him,' promised Emma. 'I just want to see him once more, that's all.' It was only now that she fully realised just how much she had come to care for the child. He was so good and cheerful, asking little and actually demanding nothing. Like a puppy, he was perfectly content if people would be kind to him; he seemed to want nothing more as yet. Perhaps he would change with the passing of the years.

Very softly Emma eased the nursery door open and took a few silent steps into the room, scarcely breathing in case even that should waken the little boy. She glanced at the bed—and her heart seemed to miss several beats before leaping right up into her throat.

The bed was empty, the covers thrown back.

She ran as fast as her legs would carry her and was panting when she entered Louise's bedroom.

'He's gone!' she gasped. 'Louise—Jeremy's not in his bed!'

'He's—' Louise seemed not to be able to comprehend. 'What are you talking about? Of course he's in his bed.'

'Would I be in this state if he—*Louise, he is not in his bed!*'

Dazed, Louise could only stare, then shake her head as if to clear it. But then she was galvanised into life and rushed out and along to the nursery, Emma hard on her heels.

'It's possible that he's—he's b-been kidnapped.' Louise turned an ashen face to her sister. 'Paul's a very wealthy man—all the Fanchettes are rich—'

'I don't suppose it's as serious as that,' broke in Emma who, with the first shock wearing off, deduced that, somehow, Jeremy had learned of Louise's going and had run off somewhere. Most likely he would be in the garden.

'We'll have to tell Paul,' was the first thing she

said. 'And then we'll all have to search—we can't catch that plane if he's not found in the next half hour or so. I couldn't leave here not knowing what's happened to him.'

'Nor could I. . . .' Louise was frowning and despite the urgency of the situation she was hesitating so that Emma in her impatience said shortly, 'What's wrong, Louise?'

'I don't want to tell Paul, not yet,' she added hurriedly as Emma would have interrupted. 'He'll be furious, and put all the blame on me. Let's, you and I, go out into the garden first and look around. We might just find him, and Paul could be kept in ignorance of the little episode.'

'I don't like that idea at all. The more people joining in the search, the better.'

'But we don't know if Jeremy's actually missing. He might just have been unable to sleep and decided to wander off into the gardens.'

'He's never done it before, I reckon?'

Louise shook her head.

'No, never—but there is always a first time.'

Emma shook her head impatiently.

'I'm convinced that he's learned of your leaving him, and he's upset. Paul must be told.'

'Can't we just have one little search on our own?' begged Louise, and after a moment's hesitation Emma agreed, albeit very much against her will.

They separated on reaching the grounds and arranged to meet twenty minutes later. A wind was blowing, and Louise said it might be a prelude to a hurricane.

'They have them occasionally,' she added, glancing up at the darkened sky. 'I've experienced one, and it started with a wind of this force.'

They parted, and Emma's fears became acute with every unsuccessful minute that passed. She and Louise had arranged to call loudly if either of them came upon the little boy, and so Emma knew that her sister was being no more successful than she. And when ten minutes had gone by, Emma's fears were so heavy upon her that they lay like an aching, leaden weight in the pit of her stomach. For now Louise's mention of kidnapping continually flashed into her consciousness as the minutes seemed to stretch to hours in her search of the grounds.

The wind was howling in the trees now, and trunks were swaying; the sea was roughening up and even the lagoon appeared treacherous.

Emma would never know what led her onto the beach, because the entire semicircle was visible from the chateau grounds. Yet her footsteps turned in the direction of the sea even while one part of her brain chided her for this waste of time. The child was nowhere to be seen. . . .

Emma's breath caught suddenly in her throat, and she felt that every vestige of colour had drained from her face. A cry . . . her eyes scanned in the ever-increasing darkness, for the moon was totally obscured now. Her attention was transferred to the sea, even though the cry seemed not to come from there.

And then she saw it! A small dark shape scarcely discernible and seeming to be lifeless . . . in the water.

'Oh, God—!' Emma choked on the words, heart

thudding wildly against her rib cage. 'Jeremy!' No, perhaps it wasn't him . . . but that little cry . . . it must be him! 'Please God let him be alive!' She had started to run and on and on she went, eyes dilated as she fixed them on the dark shape, never for a second letting it out of her vision. Fear lent speed to her limbs, but her heart was almost bursting, her lungs aching and heavy, and in her chest an excruciating pain. When after an eternity she was opposite the shape, she saw movement, and her whole body sagged with relief. The pitiful little cry again; and without more ado she stripped off her dress and underskirt and leapt into the water, swimming towards the shape—not as strongly as she would have wished but she was breathless even before she entered the water, and now the wind was also hampering her progress as she was, of course, swimming against it. Waves seemed to bury the small body, but it appeared again, and at last she reached it, almost spent herself.

'You're all right now, darling. . . .' She spoke soothing words in response to the child's whimpering. He seemed to have been holding on to a point of rock rising from the coral. Mauritius was a volcanic island almost surrounded by coral reefs, and here and there, at the far end of this particular beach, the volcanic rocks did appear.

Emma had never had any kind of tuition in lifesaving, but the rescue of a small child like this needed no expert knowledge; and she was soon swimming towards the shore, taking it slowly, praying that Jeremy would not struggle—though she doubted he had the strength—and also that her own ebbing strength would hold out. Naturally, questions whirled about in her mind as to how the child had come to be in the water. But soon she was concentrating fully on the task in hand, for the wind was now treacherous in a different way: it was carrying her sideways, so increasing the distance from the shore. It was also causing the water in the lagoon to heave, and Emma, with her gradually failing strength, began to wonder if she would ever make it to the shore. Fear rose to block her throat; wildly, she thought she should have turned back after seeing the shape in the water and shouted to her sister before attempting the rescue. Or perhaps she should have stayed by that spiral of rock and clung to it, hoping that eventually help would come. So many regrets as, practically exhausted and aware that she was crying in despair, she fought on, hampered by her burden and losing strength with every feeble stroke she made.

And then without warning the sea heaved even higher and she was being carried helplessly towards another dark shape, an ominous one this time; the rock loomed up, and the heaving sea sent her crashing against it. There was a split second of excruciating pain alongside the awareness that Jeremy was carried away, and then a great blackness descended upon her.

She fluttered her lashes and opened her eyes. Silence and only a small light . . . dazedly she tried to focus. . . . Her head! The pain. . . .

'She's coming round—oh, thank God!'

'What—?' Emma was struggling to sit up, but a firm hand pushed her back against the pillow. She opened her eyes wider as memory came flooding in and again tried to sit up. 'Jeremy!' she cried, her voice high-pitched to the point of hysteria. 'Jeremy —he's—'

'Quite safe, Emma, so lie still. You've hurt your head and the doctor's coming. He'll be here in a few minutes.' It was Paul's voice, low and hollow-sounding, as if he were very tired . . . or dejected?

'Emma—' Louise broke off, swallowing hard to clear the blockage in her throat. 'How scared I was! You were almost drowned and—'

'That'll do,' from Paul and this time the voice carried an authoritative ring. 'You can see she's going to be all right, so go and get some rest.'

Emma said weakly, 'How were we saved?'

'Paul saved you, and Pierre saved Jeremy,' said Louise who had ignored Paul's order and was still sitting beside Emma's bed. 'But it was you who really saved him. You were so brave to go into that raging sea.'

'It wasn't raging when I went in. . . .' Emma tailed off weakly then asked the time.

'Half-past ten,' from Paul who had laid a hand upon her brow. 'Is the pain very bad?' So kind the voice, and gentle . . . but yet there was something underlying that was unfathomable. 'My mind is muddled,' thought Emma then answered Paul's question.

'It aches dreadfully . . . but I've been lucky.' Her eyes were moist. It was stupid to want to cry when her life had just been saved. 'Thank you, Paul,' she quivered simply. Her hand had crept beneath the covers. She was naked and supposed it was Louise who had undressed her—not that there was much to take off, only panties and a bra. . . . The dimness was fading to blackness, and Emma drifted back into unconsciousness.

The next time she awoke the doctor was there, attending to the wound on her head.

'You're a very lucky young lady,' he said in a kindly voice. He too was a blanc Mauritian, Dr. Chastel, and had been the Fanchette family doctor for over twenty years.

'Yes,' she returned, 'I know.'

The doctor turned to Paul who was in the room, but Louise had gone.

'Get someone to make sure she has these tablets regularly; they're for the pain. It's a miracle she wasn't hurt more seriously, for that sea out there is vicious.'

When he had gone, Emma, feeling much better even though the tablets Paul had just given her could not possibly have begun to do their work, looked up into the drawn countenance above her and asked Paul to explain what had happened.

'Don't you think you should try to sleep?'

She shook her head.

'Not until I know everything.'

'Louise came to me, because you didn't turn up at the time you'd arranged to be back at the house.' He stopped and his mouth compressed. She guessed that he was angry that the two girls had not come to him immediately they discovered Jeremy was missing. However, it seemed that he considered there would be nothing to be gained by bringing that up now and he went on, 'I immediately had everyone out to join in the search. It seemed that as you were missing also, you must have found Jeremy—that was the logical explanation that occurred to me. Pierre happened to join me as I went out onto the beach; it was a forlorn hope, since I could see the whole bay in spite of the darkness. However, Pierre and I eventually did see you, just as you were being carried along. . . .' He paused and Emma saw that little beads of perspiration were standing out on his forehead.

She said, speaking her thoughts aloud, 'It must have been terrible for you, wondering if Jeremy were alive, seeing that your sister and her husband had put him in your charge.'

He looked down at her in silence, his face unmoving except for the pulsing of a nerve in his cheek. Yes, she thought, he must have been almost out of his mind with worry about his nephew.

He said at length, 'I did worry about you as well, you know.' There was censure in the tone . . . and again that something else.

'Of course. I'm sorry. You would all be worrying about me.'

'I came for you, as Louise said, and Pierre saved Jeremy.'

'I was lucky—and so was Jeremy.' She was still a little dazed and knew she had left some things out, questions she ought to be asking. One came to her and she wanted to know how Jeremy got himself into the water.

'He said he'd gone paddling—'

'Paddling! But he never leaves his bed once he's in it—' Emma broke off but added after a small hesitation, 'Had he learned that Louise was leaving him?'

Paul nodded his head.

'Sarogni told him.' Paul's eyes were hard. 'He must have taken it to heart—'

'I didn't notice anything strange about him when I read a bedtime story to him,' broke in Emma reflectively. 'He seemed quite happy then.'

Paul was looking at her with an odd expression.

'You were in the habit of reading bedtime stories to him?'

'I enjoyed it,' was all she answered to that.

'And so would Jeremy, I'm sure.' He moved restlessly, and she half expected him to bring the conversation to a close. She felt she would be able to sleep, because the tablets had been effective, and the pain was almost gone.

'If Jeremy had an affection for you then *your* going would add to his unhappiness. He must have been confused and very upset. He said when questioned that he couldn't sleep and wanted to ask you both to stay, but he went outside instead and apparently wandered about for a while. What made him go into the water will remain a mystery, since all he'll say is that he decided he wanted a paddle. The lagoon is normally almost still, and in any case Jeremy can swim, as you know. And while I'd not consent to his going in the water alone, I'm sure he'd have come to no harm if it hadn't been for the weather. He was carried out, he said, and when he found himself near the rock, he clung to it. He very clearly remembered your going to him there.'

'So that's the explanation,' mused Emma. 'It just goes to show how unpredictable young children are when their minds become upset in any way. It behooves parents always to keep a wary eye open, doesn't it?' She was very serious and thoughtful and failed to notice the almost convulsive movement of Paul's mouth, or the pulsing of that nerve again. But she did hear him give a deep sigh and asked if he were tired.

But before he could answer, Pierre came into the room to ask Emma how she felt.

'I feel much better now the pain's gone,' she answered, wondering where Eileen was.

'We have you to thank for the fact that Jeremy is alive.'

'But it was you who saved him in the end.'

'It would have been too late to save him if you hadn't done your part first,' he was quick to remind her. 'You risked your own life—'

'There didn't seem to be any risk at first,' she interrupted, embarrassed by what Pierre was saying. 'In any case, in that kind of emergency anyone would have acted as I did. You do so automatically and think afterwards. I knew I ought to have called to Louise, for that was what we had planned to do if either of us found Jeremy.

'Well, all's well that end's well,' he quoted, 'and as long as you're both going to be all right then that's all that matters.' He stayed for five minutes or so and then left.

Paul said that Emma must call if she needed anything in the night. 'Louise is next door and I'm only just along the corridor.' For some incomprehensible reason his mouth tightened and he added, 'But I suppose I shall be the last person you'd want.'

Her head shot up off the pillow then dropped again.

'Why should you say a thing like that?' she wanted to know.

'It doesn't matter.' His voice had a bitter edge to it, and Emma frowned in puzzlement. He said good night, but as he reached the door she asked, 'When shall I be able to go home? Did the doctor tell you how long I must stay here?'

'A few days,' shortly and with his hand reaching out for the doorknob. 'Don't worry about a thing.'

'You mean—the air tickets. I suppose we can get a refund.'

'We'll talk about it later,' he returned brusquely and went out.

He was in a very strange mood, thought Emma as she stared at the closed door. Oh, well, she had never been able to understand him so this was nothing new. She was sleepy but able to think, and the more she dwelt on the fact that she had been here only two weeks, the more she wondered how so much could have happened. The intimacy that had come between Paul and herself . . . but of course that could be explained by his behavior towards her; he had wanted her for his lover and made no bones about it. And when he at last had to accept defeat, he'd treated her with near indifference. But at the dinner dance he'd changed his mood even yet again, admonishing her for becoming friendly with the two young men. Not Louise, she now recalled, and yet Louise was at that time in his employ whereas Emma was not. So why chastise her and not her sister? It did not make sense at all.

Another thing that had puzzled Emma was his change of mind about taking her and Louise to the airport after saying he would. It was not as if he had been going out or had any other reason for his change of mind.

Emma's eyelids began to droop; she reached to snap off the bedlight then eased herself down beneath the covers, gingerly so as not to move her head too much. Within three minutes she was asleep.

Chapter Ten

Louise was there when Emma opened her eyes to the golden sun slanting through a chink in the drapes. She blinked several times, endeavouring to recall and concentrate.

'So you're awake. I've only just this moment come in to see if you're all right.' Louise's cool hand was on Emma's forehead. 'How are you feeling?'

'Much better; I haven't any pain.' She knew that part of her head had been shaved in order that the wound could be dressed. 'How is Jeremy?'

'As lively as a cricket. He seems to have forgotten the incident already. He's with Sarogni, eating a hearty breakfast.'

'Mother,' said Emma swiftly as her thoughts became more clear. 'She'll—'

'I phoned her just after Paul brought you in—'

'What excuse did you make for our not coming? You didn't tell her of the accident, I hope?'

Louise was oddly silent for a space. She looked troubled, and Emma's nerves tensed as she waited for her to speak.

'As a matter of fact I didn't speak to Mother. Mrs. Grant answered the phone—'

'Her next-door neighbour? Is—is something wrong?'

'Mother's ill—a very bad attack of flu but tummy trouble as well. She's been in bed for three days, and there doesn't seem to be any sign of improvement. I had intended telling Mother that there'd been some mistake about the flight we were supposed to get, but we'd be home as soon as possible. However, as I said, I didn't speak to Mother.'

'Is it serious?' Emma felt she must go home in defiance of the doctor's order that she must stay in bed for a few days.

'Seems so. But an equally worrying thing is that Mrs. Grant's leaving tomorrow evening for Canada to spend a month with her son and his family; so I shall have to go home without you—if I can get a flight and I only hope to heaven I can.' Louise looked exceedingly troubled about the possibility of her not being able to get a flight.

Emma said thoughtfully,

'So Mother doesn't know that we're not coming home together—' She stopped, a determined light in her eyes. 'I'm coming with you, Louise!'

'I'd not be too sure, Emma. It would be unwise to

travel if the doctor doesn't give his permission—please let me finish,' she went on as Emma would have interrupted. 'If I can get a flight then I shall be home before Mrs. Grant leaves, but if not—I have asked Mrs. Grant to get a nurse in—'

'But Mother will be worried out of her mind!'

'Mrs. Grant will already have told Mother the reason why we're not arriving home today. I said we'd made some mistake about the flight date—'

'That's another thing. Mother will know that's not true, because you and I would never muddle the time of anything so important as a flight. . . .' She tailed off as the door swung inwards and Paul came into the room.

'How do you feel this morning?' he wanted to know, taking up her wrist as if he were feeling her pulse.

'Much better,' was her instant reply. 'I'm going home today.'

There was a challenge in her voice which Paul completely ignored as he commented, 'Much better. Good. You will stay in bed until the doctor gives you permission to get up—'

'I don't require the doctor's permission!'

'Louise has been talking to me, and I have just now managed to get her a seat on this evening's flight—'

'You have?' from Louise who, mused her sister on noting her manner with Paul, had certainly acquired confidence in the last few days. 'Thank you very much. It's taken a load off my mind.'

Paul gave her his full attention for a space, and it was as if he were seeing her for the very first time . . . and forming a good impression.

Emma said, before either of the others could speak, 'Mother will be so worried if I don't go home. I don't want her to know I've had an accident.' In her anxiety she spoke without thinking and heard Paul say rather dryly as he glanced at her head, 'And if you did go home, how would you explain the head shaving and the dressing?'

She bit her lip.

'Perhaps I'd better stay—'

'There's no perhaps about it,' broke in Paul inexorably. 'You *are* staying.'

Louise shot him a glance, then transferred it to her sister. Emma had coloured up and turned her head away. If Louise had not been here she could have flashed Paul an acid retort!

Paul spoke to Louise. 'You will have to tell your mother that Emma has had an accident, but you can truthfully reassure her that not only is her injury not serious but also that she is in good hands.'

Louise nodded mechanically, an odd expression on her face.

'I shall make sure Mother's mind is put fully at rest,' she assured him, and after a moment's pause she added curiously, 'How long do you suppose it will be before my sister comes home?'

To her surprise he shrugged and said that depended entirely on the doctor. He seemed off-hand all at once, and a frown knit his brow. He spoke a few more words to her about the flight and then turned to go. Louise followed his departing figure, and now it was her turn to frown. She had been convinced, for one short moment, that Emma's chances with Paul were rather good . . . but now she was having second thoughts.

'What are you having for breakfast?' she inquired after saying she would have some tea sent up.

'Nothing much—er—a slice of toast will do. I'm not in the least hungry.' She was vexed at this delay, and yet almost at the same second came the thought that if she and Louise had left the house without her, Emma, having gone into the nursery, then little Jeremy would not be alive at this moment.

'I'll see to it, then,' she heard Louise say as she went over to draw the curtains back. 'And then I'll bring you a bowl of water to wash with.'

'That isn't necessary, Louise. I am quite able to use the bathroom.'

'Sure?'

'Absolutely.' She paused and then asked where Eileen was, as Emma felt sure the girl would not be pleased by this delay in her departure from the chateau.

'She decided to stay with her friend for a few more days, and likewise Madame Fanchette is prolonging her visit to friends.'

Emma fell silent, not too happy at the idea of all three women being away from the house. However, she hoped she could convince the doctor, when he came later this morning, that she really felt fit enough to travel with her sister this evening.

But her hopes were to be dashed; and when the doctor had gone, Emma looked at Paul, who had himself shown the doctor into her room, Louise being with Jeremy in the nursery.

'It's your doing, isn't it?' she accused even though she was not quite sure that her suspicions were correct.

'You're not fit to travel today.' There was an

incisive quality about his tone and a hard light in his eyes. He seemed hesitant for a space but then said tautly, 'There is no need for you to trouble yourself about me. I am fully aware of your opinion of me, so I'm unlikely to pay you any unwanted attention.' And with that he left her, her brows drawn together in a frown of sheer perplexity, the words repeating themselves in her mind, 'I am fully aware of your opinion of me. . . .'

Oh, well, she had told him several times that he was pompous and arrogant—Emma shook her head. There was something *more* than this in the words he had spoken with, she now realised, a thread of bitterness in their depths.

It was two days since the accident, and Emma, feeling completely fit and well, was standing by the little gate leading from the chateau grounds onto Paul's private beach, talking to Pierre. He had been walking on the shore, and there was a look of boredom on his face.

'I'm for home later today,' he announced, and Emma's nerves went tight. She and Paul alone . . . but for the servants. For the past two days she had been in bed for the most part—looked after by Ouma, another of the housemaids employed by Paul. But now she was up she must inevitably see more of Paul. . . .

'You're not waiting till your mother returns, then?' she said.

'There's no knowing when she'll be back. One never does know with my mother; she has what is called itchy feet. She always has to be on the move.'

'But she was to stay here for a week—'

'That's guarantee that she wouldn't get some other idea into her mind.' His eyes wandered to where his brother's yacht swayed gently in the water, movement caused by the trade wind breeze. 'I can't find much to do here; it isn't as if I have a business to keep me occupied, like Paul.' He looked at her head, the wound still covered with a buff-coloured dressing. 'Feeling okay?'

She smiled at him.

'Yes, thanks, I'm still feeling fine. I want to go home.'

'Then why don't you?'

She hesitated, wondering if she dared ask Paul for a loan.

'I haven't the money for my ticket,' she said at length.

He stared at her.

'You lost the other, of course, but surely Paul's going to reimburse you?'

She shook her head reluctantly, and confided,

'He hasn't offered, Pierre, and I must get back home. My mother's ill. I phoned my sister yesterday, and Mother is still very poorly.'

'You seem distressed,' he observed almost angrily. 'Have you told Paul you want to go home?'

'He knows I do. But I must admit that the doctor hasn't said I can travel. However, I feel fine, and in any case, a flight doesn't take anything out of you. You're only sitting there, and it's often possible to sleep.'

Pierre seemed puzzled and said decisively,

'I'll talk to Paul if you like? I know it's a difficult subject for you to broach to him, but I feel sure it is only an oversight on his part—not offering you your fare, I mean. He's so busy these days and spends long hours in his study. In fact,' he went on a trifle grimly, 'that's one reason I'm going home. Paul's been no company for me except at dinner. As for these past few days he's even gone back to his study afterwards.'

Emma said tentatively, 'You're sure you won't mind talking to him, Pierre? Perhaps you could mention it casually—in passing?'

He smiled at her manner and immediately reassured her.

'I'll be tactful, never fear. He won't guess that you and I have discussed the matter.'

'Thank you,' was all she said, and they parted company, Pierre to make for the house and Emma deciding to go on to the beach. But she was restless, and greatly troubled about her mother. As she felt well enough to travel, she wanted to get away soon, especially now that Pierre was leaving the chateau. For she was profoundly alive to the temptation that might be put in her way by Paul once he and she were alone. Emma was as much afraid of herself— her weakness—as she was of Paul.

So she turned back, her mind fully made up. If Pierre had not yet spoken to Paul about the air ticket, then she would do it herself.

He was out when she arrived back at the house, and she frowned in vexation. She went in search of Pierre and found him in the sitting-room, looking rather disconsolate. He had a glass in his hand, and she looked questioningly at him, for it was early in the day to be drinking brandy—and that seemed to be what the glass contained.

'Paul's gone out for the day,' he grumbled, 'and so I can't leave after all.'

'Why not?' Paul out for the day . . . this meant she could not ask him for her air fare, so she could not leave either.

'I can hardly leave without saying good-bye,' pointed out Pierre impatiently. 'It would be the height of bad manners.'

'Because you're his brother,' she murmured. 'But with me it wouldn't matter—' She broke off with a sigh. 'I wish you'd managed to catch him before he went out, so you could have mentioned the money I need.' It struck her that it might be a good idea to phone the airline, explain everything, and ask if she could travel now and pay as soon as she arrived home.

'I could lend you the money.' Pierre made the offer after watching her expression for several seconds. 'You look so worried, and it shouldn't be like that. Yes,' he added decisively, 'I'll lend you the money.'

'Oh, thank you very much, Pierre!' She might be lucky and get on this afternoon's flight, she thought . . . but she would be leaving without saying good-bye to Paul. . . .

Mrs. Morris had lost weight and colour; Emma was shocked by her appearance as she looked down into the ashen face and noticed the sunken cheeks, the dull, half-closed eyes.

There had been a slight deterioration in her condition, Louise had said when Emma arrived very early that morning. But Louise had added that the doctor was hopeful of an improvement within the next couple of days.

'The worst is almost over,' she ended, quoting the doctor's words.

'I'm so glad to have you both back.' Mrs. Morris's voice was weak, and somewhat hoarse as if she had a sore throat. 'Thank you for bringing Louise home, Emma. You're a good, sensible girl.'

Good and sensible . . . bitterness brought a twist to Emma's mouth. Not much sense in falling in love with a man like Paul Fanchette!

Once the girls were alone in the living-room, Louise naturally mentioned Paul.

'I left when he was out,' explained Emma, 'so I didn't say good-bye.'

Louise frowned.

'Did you have to do that?'

Emma shrugged.

'He'd gone off somewhere for the full day—so Pierre said. I suppose one of the servants told him because, he didn't see Paul before he left the chateau. If he had done so, he was going to ask him for the money to buy my air ticket.'

'Pierre was?' in a puzzled voice. 'But why him? Couldn't you ask Paul yourself?'

'I didn't like.' She paused. 'Paul was not at all friendly with me during those last two or three days after you left.'

'That seems strange. . . .' Louise was thoughtful, recalling incidents which had made an impression on her mind. Philanderer Paul Fanchette might have been . . . but had he met his match in Emma? 'Why should he be unfriendly towards you when you'd saved his nephew from drowning?'

'I didn't save Jeremy; Pierre did.'

'Rubbish!' snapped Louise irritably. 'You know very well that it was you! And I say again: why should Paul be unfriendly at a time when he should have been showing deep gratitude?'

'We've both agreed that he's a strange man—unpredictable.'

Louise's blue eyes were narrowed.

'I've said several times that there's something I don't understand. Have you said or done anything to which he could take exception?'

'Many a time.'

'You have?'

'We never agreed right from the first.'

'And yet you fell in love with him?' Louise's tone was dry.

'I'd rather not talk about Paul. He said he knew my opinion of him, and after that he was coolness itself.'

'Your opinion of him?' repeated Louise wrinkling her wide brow in puzzlement. 'You must have given it to him pretty strong, then?'

'I expect I did. I told him several times that he was pompous and arrogant, full of his own importance and superiority.'

'Is that all?' queried Louise and her sister blinked.

'Surely it was enough.'

'If you'd said it several times it must have lost its sting. No, there must have been some other reason for Paul's coolness.' There was a small silence and then, slowly and deliberately, 'It's my belief that Paul has seen something in you he's never seen before in any other woman.'

Emma was silent for a space, remembering the

several occasions when Paul had admitted to seeing something in her that he had never seen in a woman before. And yet he only wanted her for his mistress. . . . Did it really make sense? A sigh escaped her as even yet again she wished she could understand the complex character of the man.

Louise was speaking, saying something that made Emma's heart beat a little faster and her eyes open to their fullest extent.

'In my opinion, Emma, Paul wants to marry you.'

'Are you crazy! If he wants to marry me then he'd have proposed.' She shook her head emphatically. 'I don't know what gave you that idea, Louise, but it's stupid.'

'Think, Emma! Go over certain incidents; recollect the way he was with you, sometimes almost proprietorial in his attitude.' Louise's whole manner was one of impatience, and for the very first time she was the one who seemed older, wiser and more mature. 'At some point in your relationship you must have had a feeling that he was beginning to care for you—don't shake your head like that! Why did he keep you there, at his house. If he was totally indifferent to you, he'd have given you your air fare when he gave me mine.'

'Pierre believes it merely slipped his memory—'

'Rubbish! How could a thing like that slip his memory?' Louise shook her head. 'No, in my opinion that was his weapon; he could keep you there. . . .' She tailed off and gave a deep, impatient sigh. 'Yet he didn't propose to you, or even be friendly, you've said. I feel sure there is some very strong reason why he was so off-hand with you and yet, conversely, he couldn't bear to let you go.'

'Couldn't bear—' Although the exclamation carried disbelief, Emma was recalling incidents, as her sister told her to; and she had to admit that Louise was right when she implied that she, Emma, had suspected that Paul had begun to care for her. She looked at Louise, aware of racing heartbeats and irregular pulse. Could it be true? The signs were there, but Emma was afraid to accept them. Nevertheless she said, 'You really believe he—he had begun to—to care?'

'It should be obvious. Why else should he deliberately keep you without the money for your fare home?'

'At the time he gave you yours I wasn't fit to travel—or so the doctor said.'

'I'd like to bet that Paul asked him to say that.'

Emma said reflectively, 'As a matter of fact, I actually accused Paul of doing just that.'

'It strikes me,' commented her sister scathingly, 'that you're about as blind as they come. There were many signs that even I noticed, so you—if you'd only been alert—must have seen numerous signs. I'd bet everything I have that Paul fell in love with you—'

'Then why didn't he say so? And why didn't he ask me to marry him?'

'There's some reason for his attitude,' admitted Louise with a frown of perplexity. 'Are you sure you didn't do anything to turn him against you—no, that's not what I really mean,' she amended, and for a long moment she was lost in thought. 'He knows your opinion of him, he said. Anything else?'

'He said I needn't be afraid of any unwanted attention from him.'

Louise utterd a little impatient sound.

'Did it not strike you that he was piqued about something?'

It was Emma's turn to become thoughtful. She looked at her sister, recalling that it was she who had fallen for Paul at first, and Emma had been fearful of her reaction should she discover what was going on between Paul and herself. Now, it seemed, Louise was more than anxious to have Paul for a brother-in-law!

'I must admit,' she mused at length, 'that when Paul spoke those words about his being fully aware of my opinion of him, I did feel that there was something deeper than the actual recollection by him of things I had previously said—'

'You mean about his being pompous, etc.?'

Emma nodded her head.

'Yes, that's right. He seemed—sort of—bitter,' she mused.

'It's as I said: it had lost its sting . . . but something else stung him even deeper.' Louise looked at her and added almost forcefully, 'Can't you remember anything else you might have said to cause him to take that cool unfriendly attitude towards you?'

'No, I'm sure I never said anything else.' She gave a small sigh. 'We're just wasting time, Louise. Let's forget all about Paul Fanchette. I'm going back upstairs to Mother. I know she was asleep when we left her, but she might have wakened by now.'

Louise watched her go, steps dragging. She looked at her watch, Mauritius time was about four hours ahead of GMT. . . . It would be around ten o'clock at night there. Paul should still be up.

* * *

Just as the doctor predicted, Mrs. Morris began to improve and was soon sitting up in bed.

'It's miraculous!' exclaimed Louise as she showed the doctor to the door. 'We've nothing to worry about now?'

'Not a thing. It wasn't ever an illness that could end up in disaster,' he went on with a smile. 'But it was worrying for you girls who'd never had their mother ill before. She needs care, and a good long holiday—abroad if it can be done?'

'Emma and I might manage it,' said Louise.

'Try,' he advised. 'A complete change of scenery often works wonders.'

Emma and Louise talked about it and totalled up their savings. Emma knew that Paul would pay Pierre the money he had lent her, so she decided to forget all about it. Together the two girls had enough to give their mother a three-week holiday somewhere on the Continent; and as Emma had to go into work, Louise would be the one to accompany her mother.

Of course, Mrs. Morris objected strongly to the girls spending their savings in this way, but she was overruled. Louise, meanwhile, seemed to have something else on her mind and one day Emma said, subjecting her to a keen scrutiny, 'Is something wrong, Louise? You seem troubled these days?'

The careless shrug did not deceive Emma any more than the casual reply.

'Nothing at all. Don't know why you asked.'

Emma said slowly, 'Is it a job—I mean, are you afraid it won't be easy for you to get one?'

'I rather think I can go back to my old one. Mr.

Fleming did say at the time I left that if I didn't like Mauritius I must come back and see him.'

'Oh, good!' This at least was a problem solved, a problem that Emma had been secretly worrying about ever since Louise had decided to leave Paul's employ. 'Are you sure you haven't any other worry?' she just had to ask presently. 'I sense there is something on your mind all the time.'

'Well, there isn't, so don't fuss.' She walked out of the room with an air of impatience, and Emma stood staring after her. Something was the matter, but as once before, Emma knew without any doubt at all that she would get nothing out of her sister.

It was just over a week since Emma left Mauritius. She was back at work, but each day dragged, and the evenings even more so. She seemed to be seeing Paul during every waking hour and prayed that life would one day become interesting again. She had been so happy in her job before going to Mauritius, but now she had no enthusiasm; everything she did was a chore whether it be at work or at home. However, she was looking forward to the week-end for she was going to see her mother. Louise quite naturally was not looking for a job yet; she would do that after the planned holiday was over.

Emma drove up on the Saturday morning, starting out early so she would arrive before lunch. There was a car outside the house, and her heart gave a great lurch. Was her mother ill again? It was with some urgency that she slid from her car and rang the bell. Louise opened it, and her expression not only reassured Emma but it also puzzled her a little. For there was a very satisfied look in her eyes as she said brightly, 'Come right in, Emma. I have—'

'That car. . . .' Emma twisted her head around as she entered the small hall of her mother's house. 'I thought at first it might be the doctor.'

'No,'' said Louise slowly as she closed the door behind her sister, 'it isn't the doctor.'

'I realise that now, but whose is it?'

'We have a visitor—it's a hired car I expect,' added Louise as she stood waiting for Emma to precede her into the living-room from where voices could be heard, those of Mrs. Morris and. . . .

'Paul!' Suddenly Emma's legs felt weak, and her heart was racing madly. 'What—why—?'

'Go right in,' advised Louise, but Emma held back, her whole body trembling.

'I can't! He—' She looked at Louise through lashes that were suddenly stiff with moisture. 'How did he get here?' she quivered, holding a hand to her heart.

'By airplane, I expect—'

'Louise!'

'Sorry,' with some amusement. Louise was certainly very pleased with herself, noticed Emma. 'He's here at my invitation. If you must have an explanation, here it is.' Louise drew Emma back along the hall and spoke in a low tone. 'I rang the chateau one night, but the phone was answered by Eileen—much to my disgust.'

'But why did you phone the chateau?' asked Emma as her sister paused a moment. Louise stared at her with undisguised impatience.

'Because it was obvious that he loves you. I

wanted to know what had happened to—well—make him go off you, to put it in the modern idiom. He told me that you'd said outright to Eileen that you detested him. Did you?' inquired Louise with interest.

Emma started. She had completely forgotten saying that to Eileen, and now that it was brought to her memory she felt herself colouring up.

'Yes, I did,' confessed Emma but went on swiftly to explain, 'She'd goaded me, implying that I'd fallen for Paul, so I said I detested him—'

'You idiot. Didn't it strike you that she'd be ready to repeat anything you might say about Paul?'

'I would never have expected her to repeat it.'

'She wants the man herself, remember, and her methods of turning him off you would naturally be unscrupulous. As I said, she answered the phone and said Paul was out. I couldn't believe it and rang again the next day. Eileen again! This time she said Paul was away from home and would not be returning for several weeks. Well, that was a lie; I saw it at once so decided to keep on phoning until I did get Paul. He was blazing mad when I told him that Eileen had answered each time and said he was away. It happened that, just by chance, he was either out in the garden or had gone into town; whatever the reason, Eileen by sheer luck, answered my calls. However,' went on Louise with a narrowed and determined gaze, 'I would never have let up. The darned girl couldn't possibly answer Paul's phone for evermore! I told him you're madly in love with him and said there must be some excuse for your saying you detested him. I think you'd better go in,' recommended Louise with a sort of triumphant grin. 'He knows it was you who rang the bell just now. And I guess he's already losing his patience. He'll probably slate you good and hard before he proposes.' Louise had walked on with Emma, legs still weak, following behind. 'Mother and I are just going out—to do some shopping,' said Louise over her shoulder.

It was half an hour later and, true to Louise's prediction, Paul had given Emma a slating, his main accusation being that she ought to have recognised the signs that he was falling in love with her and, in turn, given *him* some signs. She took it all meekly for some moments and then could not help retaliating.

'I did recognise the signs, but let me jog your memory! It was as your mistress that you wanted me!'

'At first,' he admitted with a sudden frown, 'but afterwards I was glad you'd refused.'

'Then why the d—why didn't you say so?' she demanded.

'Because you never gave me the slightest clue that you cared. Oh, you were drawn to me physically,' he went on swiftly as her expression changed. 'But love. . . .' He shook his head. 'Not a sign.'

'Then you're blind!' she flashed, and Paul instantly responded with, 'That makes two of us!'

She looked at him, and the tears on her lashes were not caused by anger alone.

'If—if you've come h-here only to quarrel w-with me. . . .' She was suddenly swept into his arms, further speech effectively prevented by his kiss, and for a long time the living-room was silent except for little sighs of happiness from Emma and soft murmurings of endearment from her lover.

At last he held her from him, looked tenderly into her eyes, and asked her to marry him, adding ruefully when in husky tones she had answered him, 'Although I knew I was beginning to love you, I fought it. I enjoyed my carefree life and was most reluctant to change it. But you . . . in that first moment of looking into your eyes something happened to me. I denied it was anything more than physical attraction and told myself I'd be satisfied to have you as my mistress for a while. Yet all the time I was confused, trying to persuade you to be my mistress and yet always relieved that you'd resisted—'

'You were?' She looked up at him with a puzzled frown.

'As I've admitted, I was confused—and reluctant to give up my freedom. I was constantly resisting the deep attraction you had for me, telling myself it would pass. Then after I'd managed to be off-hand for a while, I'd find myself wanting you, desperately—'

'Hence those onslaughts,' Emma could not help submitting and received a little shake for her impudence.

'Each time,' he went on, and he was serious again, 'I wanted you to give in, and yet once the moment had passed I was glad you'd resisted me.' He looked down at her and gave a small sigh. 'I might as well have given in, but the gap between wanting a girl for my bedmate only, and wanting her for my wife, and I was taking time in bridging that gap.' Paul bent to kiss her, and his strong arms tightened around her.

'However, at last I was ready to ask you to marry me, as I felt you loved me. Then Eileen repeated what you'd said—it was a blow,' he added almost harshly. 'I knew I couldn't take you to the airport—in fact, I wanted only to keep away until you'd left—'

'You should have known I didn't mean it,' she protested, clinging tightly to him. 'I was always saying things I didn't mean.'

'About me?' Paul's eyes registered a mock-stern expression. 'Yes, I remember, and, my girl, I also remember your saying you'd not have me if I were the last man on earth. . . .' His voice faded as Emma placed the palm of her hand over his mouth.

She was laughing with her eyes, and he shook her, playfully. He took her hand from his mouth. She said, caressing his nape, 'Tell me some more—about your struggle, I mean.'

Paul laughed and said he'd told her just about everything, yet added reflectively, 'As I said, I felt I'd be satisfied with the physical side, but soon it was being bourn upon me that I wanted a true friend and companion, a confidante from whom there would be no secrets. In short, my beloved, I wanted you.'

She buried her face in his coat, too full for the moment to speak. But at last she was able to say, lifting her lovely eyes to his, 'It's a miracle, Paul. I can't believe it's really happening to me—no, I still can't believe it.'

'Nor I.' He stared at her in wonderment. 'Why should I be so lucky, after the life I've led?'

'A bachelor gay. . . .' Emma had not intended saying anything like that, and she looked at him to note his reaction, half expecting him to laugh.

Instead he said seriously, 'And you, my darling,

have put a stop to it. I love you, my precious sweetheart, forever. You trust me, dear?'

'With my life,' she answered confidently.

Paul drew her to his breast, tilted her face and possessed her lips, and once again there was silence in the room.

'Louise has been a real brick,' he was saying eventually as he and Emma sat very close together on the couch, fingers entwined. 'I take back everything I said about her.'

'It was only a crush; she soon realised that.'

'She was determined to bring us together.'

'She called me an idiot for not realising that you loved me.'

Paul laughed.

'That's exactly what she said to me as well.'

After a small pause Emma asked, 'Has Eileen left the chateau?'

'Most certainly!' There was a grim expression in Paul's dark eyes. 'I told her I was coming over to England to ask you to marry me, so she didn't need any telling to leave.'

'Your mother won't be pleased.'

He looked at her with a puzzled expression, and after a slight hesitation, Emma confessed to having overheard his conversation with his mother. He merely shrugged his shoulders and took Emma in his arms again. She leant her head against his shoulder and talked about *her* mother. When she mentioned the proposed holiday he said at once, 'Why can't she have the holiday in Mauritius? We shall want her there for the wedding in any case. She can stay as long as she likes.'

'Oh, Paul, can she?' Shining eyes were raised to his. 'She'll love the chateau and the gardens—she adores flowers and trees. I can't wait to tell her! Wherever can she and Louise have got to, I wonder?'

'I did tell them not to rush back,' admitted Paul with a wry smile. 'You see, my darling, I rather thought I would be making violent love to you—' He threw back his head and laughed at her embarrassment. 'We talked too much, I'm afraid. However, there's always another time,' he went on, still greatly amused by her blushes. 'In any case,' he added presently, 'we shall be married very shortly.' Imperious the tone all at once, and a challenge in his eyes. 'A fortnight will be long enough for you to get ready?'

'A fortnight! But—'

'We'll all fly back together in a few days,' he interrupted. 'There'll be plenty of time for you to do all the necessary preparations.'

'Paul—a fortnight! Invitations, Louise and mother . . . getting their dresses, and mine. . . .' Emma tailed off as she heard the key in the front door. Her mother was the first to come into the room; she stood there beaming at the two on the couch, sitting close, hands still clasped together.

'We're getting married in a fortnight,' Paul said, rising to his feet.

'Splendid,' approved Mrs. Morris imperturbably. 'In Mauritius, I suppose?' she added with a glance at Paul.

'Of course.'

'Then we shall have to be doing, shan't we?' Mrs.

Morris gave a big sigh of contentment and laid the large box she was carrying on a chair.

Emma said in some puzzlement, 'What have you in there, Mother?'

'My dress for the wedding—'

'Your!—' Emma gave her a stunned look. 'But—a dress for the wedding?'

'Louise told me over a week ago that you and Paul would be getting married, and so I thought I'd better look for a dress. I found a beauty—you'll love it! I had to have it shortened, and we've collected it today—oh, you can both laugh!' she went on when Paul and Emma could not contain their mirth. 'But from Louise's description of your character, Paul, I guessed that once you'd made up your mind you'd not stand for any delay. And so I wasn't going to be caught on the hop, rushing around for a dress.'

Louise came in carrying two bags filled with groceries. She looked a little flustered and said self-deprecatingly, 'Hope you don't mind, Paul—my taking things for granted?'

'Not in the least.' The dry tone was also edged with amusement. 'I imagine I said enough on the phone to convince you that I intended to marry Emma—especially after I'd told you I was catching the first available plane.'

Louise nodded her head, but murmured after a moment, and with a hint of mischief in her voice, 'Nevertheless, I daresay I was a little premature, letting Mother buy the dress. You see, Emma might not have accepted you.'

Paul looked tenderly at Emma and said softly, 'Was there any possibility of that, my love?'

'None at all,' she answered huskily. And, after a moment she added, changing the subject a little, 'Paul, if Louise could have her job back—if she wants it, that is, then Mother could stay until she leaves.'

'I've already thought of that,' he responded. 'We'll all have a discussion about it later.'

'But for the time being,' interposed his future mother-in-law, her brisk manner a cover for the happiness she was feeling, 'I wonder if you two would mind very much going into the parlour? Louise and I want to lay lunch in here.'

'We know when we're not wanted,' said Paul, casting her a perceptive, affectionate glance. 'Of course we'll go into the parlour. Call us when you want us.' And he took Emma's hand and allowed her to lead him out of the room. Her colour had heightened, and he laughed as he closed the door behind him. For a long moment he just stood looking at her, then held forth his hands.

'Come to me, my dearest,' he murmured a little hoarsely. 'Come and let me show you just how much I love you.'

The next moment he had his arms about her, his mouth covering hers in a kiss that was as tender as it was ruthlessly masterful. She felt his tongue against her lips, and parted them for it to enter, ecstasy shuddering through her at the contact with her silky flesh. His hands roved possessively, seeking, tempting, caressing all the tender, secret places, stroking her thighs, cupping her breasts; while his iron-hard body forced hers to arch, melding itself to his until it seemed they were almost as one . . . almost but not quite and at last, breathless as he held her away and said ruefully, 'You know, my love, the next fortnight is going to seem like a year.'

She agreed, but silently. Paul, understanding of her sudden shyness, just drew her close again and cradled her head upon his shoulder.

And through the silence came the faint rattle of dishes . . . and the singing voice of a woman who was feeling particularly happy.

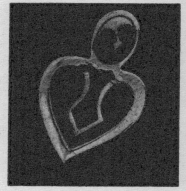

Silhouette Romance

IT'S YOUR OWN SPECIAL TIME
*Contemporary romances for today's women
Each month, six very special love stories will be yours
from SILHOUETTE. Look for them wherever books are sold
or order now from the coupon below*

$1.50 each

☐ 5 Goforth	☐ 28 Hampson	☐ 54 Beckman	☐ 83 Halston
☐ 6 Stanford	☐ 29 Wildman	☐ 55 LaDame	☐ 84 Vitek
☐ 7 Lewis	☐ 30 Dixon	☐ 56 Trent	☐ 85 John
☐ 8 Beckman	☐ 32 Michaels	☐ 57 John	☐ 86 Adams
☐ 9 Wilson	☐ 33 Vitek	☐ 58 Stanford	☐ 87 Michaels
☐ 10 Caine	☐ 34 John	☐ 59 Vernon	☐ 88 Stanford
☐ 11 Vernon	☐ 35 Stanford	☐ 60 Hill	☐ 89 James
☐ 17 John	☐ 38 Browning	☐ 61 Michaels	☐ 90 Major
☐ 19 Thornton	☐ 39 Sinclair	☐ 62 Halston	☐ 92 McKay
☐ 20 Fulford	☐ 46 Stanford	☐ 63 Brent	☐ 93 Browning
☐ 22 Stephens	☐ 47 Vitek	☐ 71 Ripy	☐ 94 Hampson
☐ 23 Edwards	☐ 48 Wildman	☐ 73 Browning	☐ 95 Wisdom
☐ 24 Healy	☐ 49 Wisdom	☐ 76 Hardy	☐ 96 Beckman
☐ 25 Stanford	☐ 50 Scott	☐ 78 Oliver	☐ 97 Clay
☐ 26 Hastings	☐ 52 Hampson	☐ 81 Roberts	☐ 98 St. George
☐ 27 Hampson	☐ 53 Browning	☐ 82 Dailey	☐ 99 Camp

$1.75 each

☐ 100 Stanford	☐ 114 Michaels	☐ 128 Hampson	☐ 143 Roberts
☐ 101 Hardy	☐ 115 John	☐ 129 Converse	☐ 144 Goforth
☐ 102 Hastings	☐ 116 Lindley	☐ 130 Hardy	☐ 145 Hope
☐ 103 Cork	☐ 117 Scott	☐ 131 Stanford	☐ 146 Michaels
☐ 104 Vitek	☐ 118 Dailey	☐ 132 Wisdom	☐ 147 Hampson
☐ 105 Eden	☐ 119 Hampson	☐ 133 Rowe	☐ 148 Cork
☐ 106 Dailey	☐ 120 Carroll	☐ 134 Charles	☐ 149 Saunders
☐ 107 Bright	☐ 121 Langan	☐ 135 Logan	☐ 150 Major
☐ 108 Hampson	☐ 122 Scofield	☐ 136 Hampson	☐ 151 Hampson
☐ 109 Vernon	☐ 123 Sinclair	☐ 137 Hunter	☐ 152 Halston
☐ 110 Trent	☐ 124 Beckman	☐ 138 Wilson	☐ 153 Dailey
☐ 111 South	☐ 125 Bright	☐ 139 Vitek	☐ 154 Beckman
☐ 112 Stanford	☐ 126 St. George	☐ 140 Erskine	☐ 155 Hampson
☐ 113 Browning	☐ 127 Roberts	☐ 142 Browning	☐ 156 Sawyer

$1.75 each

☐ 157 Vitek	☐ 170 Ripy	☐ 183 Stanley	☐ 196 Hampson
☐ 158 Reynolds	☐ 171 Hill	☐ 184 Hardy	☐ 197 Summers
☐ 159 Tracy	☐ 172 Browning	☐ 185 Hampson	☐ 198 Hunter
☐ 160 Hampson	☐ 173 Camp	☐ 186 Howard	☐ 199 Roberts
☐ 161 Trent	☐ 174 Sinclair	☐ 187 Scott	☐ 200 Lloyd
☐ 162 Ashby	☐ 175 Jarrett	☐ 188 Cork	☐ 201 Starr
☐ 163 Roberts	☐ 176 Vitek	☐ 189 Stephens	☐ 202 Hampson
☐ 164 Browning	☐ 177 Dailey	☐ 190 Hampson	☐ 203 Browning
☐ 165 Young	☐ 178 Hampson	☐ 191 Browning	☐ 204 Carroll
☐ 166 Wisdom	☐ 179 Beckman	☐ 192 John	☐ 205 Maxam
☐ 167 Hunter	☐ 180 Roberts	☐ 193 Trent	☐ 206 Manning
☐ 168 Carr	☐ 181 Terrill	☐ 194 Barry	☐ 207 Windham
☐ 169 Scott	☐ 182 Clay	☐ 195 Dailey	

$1.95 each

☐ 208 Halston	☐ 213 Dailey	☐ 218 Hunter	☐ 223 Summers
☐ 209 LaDame	☐ 214 Hampson	☐ 219 Cork	☐ 224 Langan
☐ 210 Eden	☐ 215 Roberts	☐ 220 Hampson	☐ 225 St. George
☐ 211 Walters	☐ 216 Saunders	☐ 221 Browning	
☐ 212 Young	☐ 217 Vitek	☐ 222 Carroll	

—#226 SWEET SECOND LOVE, Hampson
—#227 FORBIDDEN AFFAIR, Beckman
—#228 DANCE AT YOUR WEDDING, King
—#229 FOR ERIC'S SAKE, Thornton
—#230 IVORY INNOCENCE, Stevens
—#231 WESTERN MAN, Dailey

—#232 SPELL OF THE ISLAND, Hampson
—#233 EDGE OF PARADISE, Vernon
—#234 NEXT YEAR'S BLONDE, Smith
—#235 NO EASY CONQUEST, James
—#236 LOST IN LOVE, Maxam
—#237 WINTER PROMISE, Wilson

6 brand new Silhouette Special Editions yours for 15 days–Free!

For the reader who wants more…more story…more detail and description…more realism…and more romance…in paperback originals, 1/3 longer than our regular Silhouette Romances. Love lingers longer in new Silhouette Special Editions. Love weaves an intricate, provocative path in a third more pages than you have just enjoyed. It is love as you have always wanted it to be—and more —intriguingly depicted by your favorite Silhouette authors in the inimitable Silhouette style.

15-Day Free Trial Offer

We will send you 6 new Silhouette Special Editions to keep for 15 days absolutely free! If you decide not to keep them, send them back to us, you pay nothing. But if you enjoy them as much as we think you will, keep them and pay the invoice enclosed with your trial shipment. You will then automatically become a member of the Special Edition Book Club and receive 6 more romances every month. There is no minimum number of books to buy and you can cancel at any time.

READERS' COMMENTS ON
SILHOUETTE ROMANCES: